BEST MICROFICTION

2019

Series Editors
Meg Pokrass, Gary Fincke

Guest Editor
Dan Chaon

BEST MICROFICTION 2019
ISBN: 978-1-949790-06-1
eISBN: 978-1-949790-07-8

Layout and book design by Mark Givens
Cover illustration by Terry M. Givens

First Pelekinesis Printing 2019

For information:
Pelekinesis
112 Harvard Ave #65
Claremont, CA 91711 USA

ISSN 2641-9750

www.pelekinesis.com

Best
Microfiction
2019

Best Microfiction Anthology Series

Series Editors
Meg Pokrass, Gary Fincke

Guest Editor
Dan Chaon

Contributing Editors
Robert Scotellaro, Miles Bond, Steven John

Administrative Support
Sherry Morris

Layout and Design
Mark Givens

Cover illustration
Terry M. Givens

CONTENTS

MICRODUCTION

DAN CHAON

There is a poem by Howard Nemerov that I like called "Because You Asked about the Line Between Prose and Poetry." The poet observes as drizzle turns into pieces of snow:

There came a moment that you couldn't tell.
And then they clearly flew instead of fell.

I'm not at all interested in whether there's a line between poetry and prose, but I recognize in Nemerov's metaphor a feeling that writers and readers both know—the abrupt but imperceptible transformation from falling to flying, the lifting out of our selves. It's what we all long for when we turn to a story: that spark of becoming alive in a new body, that sensation when words on a page become a real place in our heads.

This awakening—this dream—seems to happen unbidden: at some inexplicable point we stop reading words and we begin to "see" the scene in our mind's eye, our consciousness of the physical world around us dims and we travel—apparate?—into a space that some stranger has imagined for us: we've been given a flying piece of snow that we can inhabit, but neither reader nor writer is fully in control of where it will take us to.

Is the text a horse that the reader rides, a train that the reader boards? Or does the story inhabit and transmogrify the reader, does the reader blossom into a piece of snow spontaneously, without choosing? We say we were "sucked in," "transported," "caught up"—but by what? With whom are we collaborating when we read a story that enthralls us?

For me, the most exciting thing about microfictions is that they draw us starkly into that complex state of collaboration between reader and writer, that space that is both shared and private, scripted and spontaneous.

Take, for example, the famous six-word story, "For Sale: Baby Shoes, never used." It is only a template, a blueprint that allows readers to recreate scenes in their mind: *Where are the baby's shoes being sold? Who is selling them? Why were they never used?* Each reader will have a different answer, but all of the answers are correct.

I can't say whether I fell into the stories in this volume, or whether they caught me up and carried me off, whether I'm reading them or they're reading me. They are glimpses, shadows, Rorschachs. Hopefully, they'll possess you.

FOREWORD
MEG POKRASS, GARY FINCKE
Series Co-Editors

Gary Fincke

Twenty years ago, I was looking for a way to jump-start my freshman Intro to Fiction workshops. A colleague handed me "Black Tickets" by Jayne Anne Phillips and said, "Take a look at the short ones." I did, and my workshops were all the better for it. The "short ones," not much more than a page long, were intense and immediate, but above all, they were so precisely observed that a memorable story was created in several hundred words. Having those students try to write such stories became how my freshman fiction workshops began. It was nearly magical how quickly they understood that closely observed character, place, and situation could generate the tension necessary for story.

No surprise. For the past seven years, the program I directed has offered workshops exclusively for writing short form fiction. It has been exciting to see widespread enthusiasm among students, the kind I have for Luke Wortley writing in reverse chronology in "Reverse Field Trip," with its movement from catastrophe through each detail that accounts for it, each one more innocent and small, until the reader is heartbroken with the burden of foreknowledge. Or the brief, compelling "The Chemistry of Living Things" by Fiona J. Mackintosh, how she moves from the details of sedatives muting the ordinary world to a moment of wonder seeing the natural world up close. And Sharon Telfer's "My Father Comforts Me in the Form of Birds" constructed through a retrospect of birds to show the qualities of comfort a deceased father has instilled in the narrator's life.

It has been a joy to co-edit *Best Microfiction 2019* and introduce readers to a new "best of" anthology, one that celebrates the compression and exactitude that drives each of these stories straight to the heart.

Meg Pokrass

When I began writing flash fiction, there were only about twelve literary magazines that would even considering publishing something as short as a few hundred words. That was in 2009. Today, in 2019, there are thousands of literary magazines which are asking for flash submissions: many journals actually prefer these pieces to traditional length short stories. The form is now commonly taught in university creative writing courses and has redefined the indie lit scene.

I am amazed by the quality of the work that has recently appeared: stories such as "Fragments of Evolution" by twenty-two year-old writer Cavin Gonzalez, whose voice is so fresh, creative, and true it makes me cry. The chill of unspoken tragedy in Melissa Goode's "Empire of Light"— a masterful example of how what is not said can feel so much bigger than what is. The painfully visceral torture of an innocent in Sarah Arantza Amador's story, "Sanctus Spiritus, 1512."

After reading a year's worth of stories for this anthology, it is clear to me that there is no formula for success. No "trick". A winning micro must be innovative and inventive, told in a way that only that particular author can tell it. As with all good writing, it must come from the heart. These eighty-seven ingenious stories remind me of why it is the form I most love.

SANCTUS SPIRITUS, 1512

SARAH ARANTZA AMADOR

They brought her down the mountain the afternoon before the earth shook and the sea retreated and then returned four times stronger and taller. It was dry winter, and the camp was bored; the captain sent a troop of soldiers to push a slave up into the hills in search of gold. The further they climbed, the more desperate they all became, and when they found her half-frozen in the icy damp of a high cave, a shock of iridescent scales and bare breasts and buttocks, they forgot about the gold completely and stole her instead. As they wound their way through the camp, people stopped and stared at the woman tightly bound in horsehair rope. She was locked into a livestock crate brought off one of the ships after she attacked a cook who had reached out to touch the opaline spines along her back, and there she sat unblinking, slow pulse, as slaves, soldiers, and mistresses alike delighted in the way she changed colors when they poked her with sticks through the bars. After the disaster, the dead were disentangled from the mangroves and piled with trash into mounds along the beaches. The camp cried and prayed, and she sat in her cage, focused on the smell of sea brine and the cook's meaty neck.

Residing in the Santa Cruz Mountains of Northern California with her dog Roscoe and person Richard, **SARAH ARANTZA AMADOR** writes about longing, ghost-making, the endearment of monsters, and the twists and turns of human loving kindness. She tweets @ArantzaSarah and sometimes blogs from www.saraharantzaamador.com.

HE, SHE, IT, THEY

ANITA ARLOV

He's graven. She's gilt. He was glass-bottle-fed. She was weaned a china doll. He cuts loose. She's unmoored. He picks her Mexican daisies. She reads him Inés de la Cruz. He's on Cloud Nine. She's Man in the Moon. He's finger inlet, bracken, orca, syrup. She's Matariki, moss, cowrie-shell, Hula Hoop. She sleeps in his spoon. He wakes her toes-first. He fries her tomatoes. She peels in the sun. He books Dunedin. She knits him a scarf. He takes on a greyhound. She collects horseshoes. He plants rosemary. She goes to pottery.

He lets slip a white lie. She grows black moons. He slaps his face. She slaps her mouth. He's power cut, sleet, cacophony, sludge. She's burnt toast, high humidity, rent increase, aerosol. He's more-pork cry. She's wild rabbit spoor. He flattens a possum. She wouldn't be caught dead. He's a slot screw. She's a Phillips driver. He's wet towels, velcro, bad breath, block-buster. She's hair-ball, silverfish, traffic fine, art house. He's Saturday. She's Friday. He's long lost tribe. She's street barbeque. He's barbed tomcat. She's treed queen. He pings a nerve. She's a live wire. He's haemochrome. She's bleached bone.

He's breast of water. She's landfall. He's tin can. She's can opener. He's focaccia, nail gun, folk lore, archipelago. She's manuka honey, neon light, kelp forest, quantum theory. He's wind gust. She's window. He's motu. She's hopscotch. He's dinghy. She's jetty. He's indigo. She's Indian Ink. He's vinyl, rope bridge, home-cooked-meal, equal pay. She's open fire, green belt, skylight, long weekend. He's paper-scissors-rock. She's tic-tac-toe. He's sober driver. She's wine on special. He hangs it out. She brings it in. He catches the backbeat. She pours on the slant. He's Battle of Britain. She's fly.

ANITA ARLOV lives in Auckland, New Zealand. She emcees Inside Out Open Mic, a monthly gig for prose writers and poets. She convened the team organising the NZ Poetry Conference & Festival 2017. "He, She, It, They" won first prize in NZ's National Flash Fiction Day Competition 2018.

KNOCK, KNOCK

JESSICA BARKSDALE

The bad childhood joke is that everyone tells one.

The bad childhood joke is that your bad childhood is yours, the thing you clutch like the doll you clutched for three years and then lost, finding it one spring under a patch of overgrown weeds. You loved that doll, despite the bugs and weather that had eaten her hair, dug out her plastic eyes, torn her dress, lost her shoes. She was found! Oh, she was found, and then your father made you throw her away, your ruined baby, your love, all that feeling for three long years you'd whispered in her rubber ear, gone.

The bad childhood joke is that you pretend it doesn't exist, closing the door on its punch line, wham. Goodbye, stupid joke. But it knocks again. Who's there?

The bad childhood joke is that your childhood wasn't all bad. There are those summers at the pool, the girls you grew up with, swimming alongside them day after summer day, girls turned women you still lean close to and whisper with.

The bad childhood joke is death made it better.

The bad childhood joke was that even when it was

better, the past hung in the house like your father's tobacco smoke. It cleared a little. You found you could breathe.

The bad childhood joke is three sisters walked into a bar. Only two walked out.

The bad childhood joke is that you tried not to tell it to your children. You told another joke. Maybe not as bad. Maybe worse. You have heard them tell it a couple of times to girlfriends, almost laughing. You tried not to cover your ears.

The bad childhood joke is expensive. You pay for it for a long time.

The bad childhood joke is the joke that keeps giving, even as you arc toward old age. It's the joke you tell best, perfecting each line down to the bone, your skeleton, the part of you that is made of light and air.

JESSICA BARKSDALE'S fourteenth novel, *The Burning Hour*, was published in 2016. Her poetry collection *When We Almost Drowned* is forthcoming from Finishing Line Press in March 2019. She is a Professor of English at Diablo Valley College in Pleasant Hill, California. She is soon to live in Vancouver, Washington with her husband and two dogs.

from KYSO FLASH

SWIMMING IN CIRCLES

ROBERTA BEARY

On the way to the morgue I pull over on the highway. The radio announcer is talking about this whale swimming with her dead calf. Whenever the calf slips off, the whale grabs it with her mouth, tosses it in the air and catches it on her nose. "Shut that stupid crap off," Becca says, "I need to see Rob's car. I need to see what happened." The VW is squeezed in half, like an accordion. We peer inside. A rose is holding up what's left of the windshield. Becca reaches out her hand. "Careful," I say, "there's a lot of broken glass in there." Becca shakes the petals into my pink handkerchief. She got one too, green to match her eyes Mom said. That was 40 years ago.

The round clock in the morgue waiting room reads 3pm. I open my purse and see the handkerchief. I unfold it and count six red petals. "Hold onto those for me," Becca says, "I can't look at them right now." A woman comes over and takes Becca's arm. When Becca comes back she says, "His hair smelled so clean. Like he just washed it." I picture cool, white cotton sheets waiting for me in my hotel room.

In the hotel bar, Becca order a double vodka. She

gives me and the bartender the long version. How Rob took a shower before he left around midnight. How the cops woke her at 4am, banging on her front door and flashing their lights. While she's talking I picture the whale tossing her dead calf up in the air. Catching it on her nose. Swimming in circles. "I keep thinking he's going to call me," Becca says, checking her phone. The bartender gives me a look and I ask for the check. Digging in my purse for my credit card, I see the handkerchief. It will be years before I throw away the petals.

ROBERTA BEARY'S micro-memoir *Now, It's Fresh Fish* was recently selected by the New York Times for its Tiny Love Stories feature. Her work also appears in *Rattle, KYSO Flash, 100 Word Story, Cultural Weekly*, and several anthologies. She and her husband live in County Mayo, Ireland.

THE HUNGERER

MATT BELL

Because the older knew no other way to keep the younger safe—not with his soft and pudgy body, his first and most-lasting source of shame—he tricked his sister into the cottage's oven, holding its door shut against her struggling, reading her her favorite Plath to soothe her to sleep. When she was warmed through and still he took her into his body with fork and knife, eating every bit of her delicious meat, gnawing every last organ, cracking bone and sucking gristle from crackling skin until his plate was empty. Afterward the older's belly hurt so that he thought he might die there at the table, but he did not die. His long life stretched achingly sad without the living company of the younger, and despite his great appetite—I'm eating for two, he cried often at his table set for one, and all the townspeople thought him a great idiot—never again was there another meal that tasted so good, not until he was in his old age, when at last he took his knife to his still-distended belly, believing his swallowed sister at last as safely grey-haired as he, at last unattractive enough to be set free, to take her place at the table of life. And from the wound he made in himself his living sister did spill—but when the younger emerged soaked in her brother's gore, the older saw she was not aged at all, but exactly as young as when he'd last seen her: a bloody maiden ready to begin at last her much-delayed adolescence, a great beauty born twice into a world the now-elderly older could never do enough to secure.

MATT BELL is the author of the novels *Scrapper* and *In the House upon the Dirt between the Lake and the Woods*, as well as the short story collection *A Tree or a Person or a Wall*. His writing has appeared in *The New York Times*, *Tin House*, *Conjunctions*, and many other publications. A native of Michigan, he teaches in the Creative Writing Program at Arizona State University.

HEALTH CARE

DICK BENTLEY

On this hill, in this clump of trees at the edge of the golf course, I sit with the wind swaying the daisies. Now distant Bernardini's milky eyes are focused on the golf ball as he bends down before putting. He studies the ground. He analyzes the lie, the turf, the wind. Bernardini is President of the Health Group that has denied me treatment. The treatment is too experimental for my tumor, the bean counters said. So I am to die. And so is Bernardini. The sun oozes across the sky; the breezes undulate over my skin. My heart beats with the systole and diastole of waves against a breakwater, and boredom creeps over me like vines. I know what I want: an event, by which I mean a squeeze of the trigger of the weapon now aimed at Bernardini's distant heart, as he kneels over his tiny white ball on the 11th hole. His golfing partners, more health care executive Pension plan investors, insurance dealers. A little acidic gossip. A little high-tech megadeath, a sharp thing that will wake them up. Then run a street sweeper over the 11th green, turn the breeze up to hurricane so the daisies' heads tear off and hurtle through the air like bullets. A melon-burst, the tomato-colored splatter, Bernardini raises his arms as he kneels as if sniffing the air. His wings are spread for flight. He's howling like a siren, and he finally has everyone's full attention, before he rolls over like a noon pigeon.

Everyone gets a turn and now it's mine. But some get more turns than others, and I've never had a turn, not one. You think I didn't hate their pity, their forced kindness. They are pointing now toward this clump of trees. I could have a few more of them by the time they sentence me to death.

I'll already be dead. You can wipe your feet on me, twist my motives around all you like, dump stones on my head and drown me in the river. What we want, of course, is nothing more than the same old story: the trees pushing out their leaves, shucking them off; the unfurling of slugs; the worms vacuuming the dirt; the daisies and their pungent slow explosions. We want it all to go on and on again, the same thing each year, monotonous and amazing.

DICK BENTLEY'S books, *Post-Freudian Dreaming, A General Theory of Desire,* and *All Rise* are available at Amazon. He won the *Paris Review's* International Fiction Award and has published over 250 works of fiction, poetry and memoir in the US, the UK, France, Canada and Brazil. Check his website www.dickbentley.com.

BIRDHOUSE
GREGORY BROWN

Pre-meeting chirrup, caw-caw. New face, old face, coffee, cigarettes. Make a circle, little nest. *What would you do if you only had one year left to live?* The addicts share out, one by one. I'd spend it with my kids, one guy says. I'd take my moms to Disneyland. Me too, me too. Definitely go travelling with my family. And on and on. Joanie's already tired of this shit, the pep and preening. Three straight days: everybody putting on their brightest feathers. Forgive, forgive. Love, love. Blah, blah, blah. She can feel the heat in her chest, the roil of bile rising up her throat, she wants to cut these motherfuckers down, show them how un-special their love. How wrong. She's seen the scars on her roommate's arms. Heard Kevin O. confess to picking through his OD'ing girlfriend's sweatpants, scoring a twoonie and a couple of crushed cigarettes. Nobody here who hasn't fucked over, been fucked over. Joanie's in her head. Time flies, but where? Then: this woman, Vola, is saying, I'd make birdhouses. *Birdhouses?* Yeah, Vola says. *You a bird lover?* No, Vola says, I don't really like birds. Scattered laughter. Vola says, I just think it'd be a nice thing to do. A small, nice thing. Vola looks down in her lap as she says this, clasping her hands. Now it's Joanie's turn to speak, but she's not sure anymore. She's forgotten something important about herself. It's flown the coop. She's thinking about a thing her parents told her when she was five or six, a lie to get her out of the house: throw salt on a bird and its wings won't work. Let you pick it up, take it home, love it. Joanie's trying to remember: did it work?

GREGORY BROWN is a graduate of UNC-Greensboro's MFA program in Creative Writing. His work has appeared in *Paragon*, *Pulp Literature*, *Tate Street*, *PRISM International*, and *The Journey Prize 30: The Best of Canada's New Writers*. He teaches at the University of Virginia's Young Writers Workshop and the Creative Writing for Children Society in Vancouver.

CANDLELIGHT AND FLOWERS

TETMAN CALLIS

"Fuck me," he said, "is one of the sweetest things I've ever heard a woman say. I don't mean a fuck me said while sitting side-by-side on a couch or while waiting on a bed for the clothes to come off—a fuck me as in let's fuck. I mean a fuck me said while she's naked on her back underneath you, her legs apart and pulled up by her hands in the crooks of her knees, her eyes closed and mouth opened, you naked and hard and pushing into her, pinning her down, and her engulfing you in the moments when the both of you are at your most powerful and your most vulnerable, while the wet spot growing in the bed underneath her is still warm and she wants to be with you, has opened her warmth and softness to you and it pleases her, *you* do, you are pleasing her, you, skinny and snaggle-toothed, helping her to reach a place inside herself where it's not about you anymore but rather it's passion and a sort of joy and courage you'll never understand and a woman who opens herself to them and is opened by them so much that she abandons fear, half-whispering to you sweet trusting words that could cause no end of trouble if you turn out to be not quite the person she thought you were when she asked you into her bed. Fuck me—it's practically I love you."

"No, it's not," she said. "It's not."

TETMAN CALLIS has published various short fictions in such magazines as *NOON*, *New York Tyrant*, *Atticus Review*, *Queen Mob's Tea House*, and *Neon Literary Magazine*, and two books, *High Street* and *Franny & Toby*. He has a degree in philosophy and lives in Chicago with his wife and their two cats.

TRAINING
MICHAEL CHIN

We signed up on the hope of gold-plated, leather-strap championship belts. The wonder of children. The lust for women who doted over biceps. All we were promised was aching bodies and misery.

We hoped we would be good. Naturals from day one.

We hoped to learn how to make pulled punches, inverted top-rope hurricanranas, and cross-face chicken wings look devastating without anyone getting hurt. The first lesson promised something to the contrary. Promised *everyone* would get hurt.

He stretched us. Hammerlocks and full nelsons and neck cranks. Then the chokes, one-by-one, putting us to sleep.

We didn't sleep much. Four to a room, two bare mattresses that were stained with blood, that smelled like feet, that were all too small for two men's bodies. So half of us slept on the floor—the losers of arm wrestling matches and rock-paper-scissors contests.

Some quit.

We bruised and bled and scarred and got staph infections. A few of us cried, but not as many as would have were the penalty not an extra half hour of *training*—enduring Romero specials, wind sprints until we hurled, Hindu squats until our piss ran red.

We turned ankles and dislocated shoulders and kept on until we had fractures kept on until we hurt permanently.

Some quit.

We learned to give and receive fireballs, Memphis style. Fireballs that singed our eyebrows and left rippling wounds over our eyelids.

Some quit.

We dove. In the ring, body to body, then off the top rope to the floor. *Won't we die?* Only a few of us thought to ask.

To be one of us, the trainer said, *you have to give up your life.*

So do we quit now?

We who carried on—we few—we hoped we might be legends.

We were promised nothing.

MICHAEL CHIN was born and raised in Utica, New York and currently lives in Georgia with his wife and son. He authored the full-length short story collections *You Might Forget the Sky was Ever Blue* from Duck Lake Books and *Circus Folk* from Hoot 'n' Waddle. Visit him at miketchin.com.

EUTHANASIA
MYFANWY COLLINS

1.

Our bedspread was a patchwork quilt my friend made for me. She met a man in Montreal who practiced acupressure. They lay down in the field beside my house and he found the points necessary to abort their fetus. Once she and I picked up a hitchhiker outside a prison and drove him to the ferry. You were on an overnight at work and didn't know, wouldn't have known until much later if he had killed us. The city had seven hills. Just like Rome. But not. I sat in the kitchen wrapped in the quilt and worked. Then you fucked your coworker and told me you loved her. I threw my Pelican Shakespeare at your head and missed but broke the book's spine. Later I asked for all of the details about you and her and ate them greedily as they spilled from your mouth.

2.

The way you twitched in the car. Your tic. The way you smelled the inside of books when you were reading them. The way you said I didn't understand about collecting vinyl, like it was some art. Science.

Magic. Your missing tooth. The thick pelt of hair in your ears. Your ex-wife saying to me, I know it feels good to have someone crazy about you. I said, no, it feels horrible. It feels scary. Then I realized you were all in it together.

3.

The man across from me made art out of solder. His hands never touched the table, sticky with spills, before the seisiún. And your outrage and your pride. It was about those, too. When we put the dog down. When we euthanized the dog. When we killed the dog. The second after he stopped breathing. The second he stopped breathing. I said, "I want him back. Bring him back to me. My friend. My friend." All of my ugliness and my shame. That does not exist here.

4.

Your hands around my neck. It would have been easy to have been killed. I realize that now.

MYFANWY COLLINS is the author of two novels and a collection of short stories. She lives, works, teaches, and writes in Massachusetts.

NORTHERN LIGHTS

TIM CRAIG

After an hour or so, I decided to ask him about the tooth.

It was dangling from the sun visor on a piece of cotton, and it had a gold filling that occasionally glinted as we passed under the lights.

The lorry driver reached up and flicked it with his fingernail, setting it dancing back and forth.

"It was my father's," he said.

Then he grinned.

"The only gold I ever got from him."

Pavel turned to look at the road ahead, his expression serious once more. All three lanes were busy with traffic heading north for the weekend.

He was quiet for a moment or two, then he shrugged.

"He hit my mother, I hit him. He left. I never saw him again.

"I was seventeen."

He flashed the headlights to allow a Sainsbury's lorry to pull back into the inside lane. The lorry moved across, then toggled its indicators in thanks.

"I found the tooth two days later. It had landed in a flowerpot and I thought I'd better take it with me in case another evil old bastard grew out of it."

He smiled, and as he did so I noticed a sparkle of gold in his own mouth.

Neither of us said much more after that, and he dropped me off at the next services.

After he'd gone, I stood for a while on the motorway bridge, watching the trail of diamonds and rubies on the wet tarmac.

TIM CRAIG (UK) works as a freelance copywriter and translator. In 2018, he won the Bridport Prize for Flash Fiction and placed third in the Bath Flash Fiction Award. Originally from Manchester, he now lives in Hackney in East London with his wife and three children.

YOU'VE STOPPED

TOMMY DEAN

You've stopped asking me to marry you. I think, finally, this is a good thing. We're the last people on Earth, you cry into my ribs, your nose stopping on each ridge of bone like a gate unlatching. We don't know that's true, I say, but the air in this bunker is getting heavy with our foul-smelling humidity. We're just springs rebounding and recoiling, thrusting our hands out in the dark, mauling the air, waiting to connect.

You've stopped gorging on top ramen and bubble gum. The floor is littered with wrappers, slick with noodles, and those little peas that cling to the bottom of my shoes. I keep them on because I can't give up the idea of running, my calves refusing to give up, the muscles popping and stretching below me, warning of attrition. There's nowhere to run, I whisper, punching them twice a day anyway. You do love me, you say, mistaking my regrets as compliments.

You've stopped checking the latch on the containment door. The fear of being invaded has become the trampled dust, the network of shoe imprints you trace across the floor, pacing to keep the edge of possibility fresh in your mind. This you refuse to stop, coming closer and closer to my hip, my knees. Proximity, when we lived above, often created desire. But now you dart, zig and zag like a goldfish in too small of a bowl. I miss your skin by millimeters.

You've stopped talking, your voice caking over with fallen dust motes because you refused to wear the hospital masks I had provided. Then how will we kiss, you asked at my first suggestion. Survival, at first, felt flirty, like finding ourselves alone in a hotel while everyone else was at the beach. Now, I'm pretty sure the beach doesn't exist. You still assume the world is out there, waiting for us, that we've merely stepped off the page of this fairy tale you've been writing in your head.

You've stopped waking up unless prodded by my fingers checking your neck for a pulse. A bear in hibernation, eyelids caked in allergy and lethargy. Even your heart has slowed. I whisper I love you, a hundred times a day, seizing on the lightning bug blip of your heart as it pushes back against my palm, its own failing cadence letting me know that I'm too late.

TOMMY DEAN lives in Indiana with his wife and two children. He is the author of a flash fiction chapbook entitled *Special Like the People on TV* from Redbird Chapbooks. He has been previously published in the *BULL Magazine*, *The MacGuffin*, *Split Lip Magazine*, *Spartan*, *Hawaii Pacific Review*, and *New Flash Fiction Review*. Find him @TommyDeanWriter on Twitter.

MR ROCHESTER AND I

OLGA DERMOTT-BOND

have come to an agreement of late. I sit with him and his dog until the small hours; faces, hands, paws gleaning the last of the embers' glow whilst Thornfield darkens around us in the gloom. I've told him that I have always thought him ridiculous, some repressed Victorian fantasy dreamt up in Charlotte's cold narrow bed. He didn't reply. Once I even tried to explain the fact I'm feminist and the many reasons why *The Wide Sargasso Sea* is a really great book. Silence.

But here we are, sitting together, waiting to see if we can forget our moulded, knotted, tangled selves, listening for the creaking rafters high above. He reads a book and I stare into the coals. Mr Rochester and I spend most evenings like this now, whilst Jane sleeps innocently and Bertha stalks late. He doesn't seem to mind me coming—words choke my throat into sobs these days, thoughts breaking up like a boat in a storm, so best not to utter any.

So, our mistakes lick the dusty hearth every night and we stay silent, covering up our attic-hearts that beat stubbornly, on and on and on. Mr Rochester and I sense that loneliness can escape, even if we pay someone to keep it locked up. Mr Rochester and I know that, soon, all the pain and the past we want to bury will find a way of coming out, of growling, screaming, until it tears our hair out from the roots. Mr Rochester and I have come to an understanding that love will find us, blind us and burn down our houses in the end.

OLGA is originally from Northern Ireland and lives in Warwickshire. A former Warwick Poet Laureate, she has had poetry and flash fiction published in a wide range of magazines. Last year she was one of the winners of the BBC Proms poetry competition, and was shortlisted in The Poetry's School Primers competition. @olgadermott

FIRE, OCEAN
LEONORA DESAR

My father comes from fire. At night I can hear his steam, twisting his irises into candlewicks. My mother stands in doorways, watching.

Come to bed, Jeff, my mother says. Just a minute, Rhonda, my father says.

He dials up the Phil Collins, paces. Dad loves his Phil Collins. He also loves Britney Spears and bad kung fu movies and slipping cigarettes to my friends, slipping and lighting them with his tongue, "like magic." Did I mention we're 16?

The music dims. My father sits. This is the worst, his blue-black silence. The house rocks in his slow burn, rocks and rocks. I imagine him gone, Mom hosing down the place in a pair of red stilettos. She pretends she doesn't see—the handprints flaming down his back, those teeth marks from other women.

My mother comes from water. She is the pair of cool hands that coax my father from burning rooftops, her body the safety net he falls into at the bottom. He sees her most in absence—the laundry that doesn't get done, the rind of soap that hardens in the bathtub drain when she leaves to visit Aunt

Linda for a week. She dissolves in corners, watches my father parade in restaurants. His fire melts her, disappears her inside his body.

I am the smoke that comes from my father's flame. I whistle out of windows and coil down the stairs. I slip shapeless into dive bars. I let wannabe married rock stars feel me up in bathroom stalls and gutters. I am my mother's ocean. I am her water, bending to Bowie on the jukebox, to the smell of weed and wedding rings and to long, blue bodies, to what they want, to what they tell me to do, against the wall or over a graffitied toilet, to lips and thighs and hands. I am the mist they wash off lips and thighs and hands. I let them do what they want.

MY FATHER'S GIRLFRIEND
LEONORA DESAR

My father's girlfriend had a secret ring. She had many. It was a dial tone when they first met. They didn't need words, he could just pick up the phone, and they would know each other. He stood there and twisted the cord, and the perfume came, it wrapped around his neck. It smelled like cognac and blueberries. It smelled like cashmere.

It was two and a half when she wanted him to fuck her. Two long rings and a fast one. The first two were a slow deep kiss, the half was a peck, it meant, get over here. When they were fighting it was just a peck, there were three of them. Sometimes I could see a bird flying across the room. She pecked at my father, and he rolled his eyes. My mother said, what's that, my father said, it's just a bird. She had a carrot top of hair like a mohawk. It was spiky like her eyes. She smelled like cigarettes, and she left a ring of lipstick around my father.

When she was done being fucked the ring was slow. You couldn't really hear it, but it was there, the slowness. It sounded like a woman drinking alone, the way she got up and pretended to walk straight. The slowness was the getting up, it was walking across the room. It was that moment she took looking at the phone, wondering if she should call him or my mother.

After she killed herself the phone still rang. It was slower, fainter. It smelled like lipstick, and then it was just a dial tone. My father stood there twisting the cord. The lipstick twisted all around us.

THE MONKEY
LEONORA DESAR

My husband read my diary. He says it, I read your diary. And then he takes it back. And then he says it again. He puts my diary in both hands, he is saying left, right, he is switching it up behind his back. He looks just like my grandpa. He used to do this. My grandpa, he'd put a silver dollar in his hand and switch it up. And I'd have to guess. Which hand it's in. If I got it right I kept the dollar. If I got it wrong I'd get a slap under my skirt. It would be quick, easy. It wouldn't leave a mark. My husband says it, left, right and if I guess well I'll get to keep him, my husband, I'll know that this diary thing is all a joke, like April Fools', when he said he got a monkey. He said it and it sounded real, so real I almost picked up a manual at Barnes & Noble, how to train your monkey. I imagined that monkey smell and the monkey flinging shit and my husband opening the door and caning me right on the butt. He'd do it and we'd go watch *Wheel of Fortune*. The monkey would sit between us, it would be a well-trained monkey, it would pass back the remote. But there was no monkey. There was just my husband, eating dinner. Saying sorry, babe, I hope I didn't upset you. I imagine it would be like that. It would be just like that right now.

LEONORA DESAR'S writing has appeared or is forthcoming in River Styx, Passages North, Black Warrior Review Online, Mid-American Review, SmokeLong Quarterly, and elsewhere. She won third place in River Styx's microfiction contest and was a runner-up/finalist in Quarter After Eight's Robert J. DeMott Short Prose contest, judged by Stuart Dybek.

from SOUTHAMPTON REVIEW

THE STRIP CLUB
WILL FINLAYSON

And then my brother he shows me how to stuff dollar bills into their panties, thin black lace over orange skin, pasties over nipples, and I'm thinking this is strange. But then he says "relax" but I can't relax. I cram the ones in and I'm all stiff like I'm stuffing a letter in a mailbox except it's not a mailbox it's a person like just take your damn money and my brother he says "this is it man" like he always says with that smile with the teeth. I'm looking at the girls but I'm looking at the men not hollering or reaching or slippery like I thought they would be but standing with arms crossed and staring like we were at a museum like we were admiring art. And it's hard not to think about who took my brother to a strip club for his first time and if he was sweating the first time like I am but "relax" he says and I say to myself I mean it's just like church you just sit and listen and stuff your ones in the right place but then one of the strippers falls from her pole, way high up, and lands on her head, weird though, and the guys are racing to help her and there's blood. But then the staff are pushing them away "don't touch" they're saying and that's confusing and there's blood and my brother looks at me and I know he wants to say "it's not like this" but it is "this" isn't it? This is what I'm seeing the pasties and the ones and the red matted hair and the men standing around with their hands held out in front like cowboys drawing warmth from dying coals.

WILL FINLAYSON studied poetry and fiction at BYU in Provo, Utah. His work has been published in *Inscape*, the *Southampton Review*, and *Alexandria Quarterly*.

EVEN THE CHRISTMAS TREE WAS NICER THAT YEAR

VALERIE FOX

Mama is mostly coherent. Brother Billy is nowhere to be seen, thank our lucky stars, says Charly, who watches a lot of dumb TV like *Leave It to Beaver*. Charly's sober dad appears carrying a giant cage holding a bird chick. "It's a mynah bird. It eats lizards and we can teach it to talk, a hundred words." Charly learns all about how to fix up the chick's habitat. She calls the chick Baby Jesus since it's Christmas, even though the chick is a girl.

Charly used to be Billy's sidekick, but he's been gone for almost a year even though he should be in high school. He returns unexpectedly when school would already be out, and he won't quit trying to get Baby Jesus to perch on his hand. It's not something a mynah can do. Billy tries every way he can think of, pressing his dirty fingers too tightly around Baby Jesus's small body and talking to her like he's some kind of expert at bird hypnosis.

The words fill Charly's head: *ace in the hole, billy, charly, full house baby, hello honey, hi baby, hit me up, I abhor you, let in some air, love you, mama, mustang, normal, one two three four eight, say that again, up the ante, wake up sunshine, what'dya say, where are you hiding, you are loverly, you are lost, you are my super moon you are where are you?*

VALERIE FOX'S books include *Insomniatic*, *The Rorschach Factory*, and *The Glass Book*. She recently published *The Real Sky*, which features illustrations by Jacklynn Niemiec. Much interested in collaboration, she's published poems and stories written with Arlene Ang. She co-wrote, with Lynn Levin, *Poems for the Writing: Prompts for Poets*.

from CINCINATTI REVIEW

ANY BODY
SARAH FRELIGH

Down under was your stomach, hollowed out and shouting. What it said, you didn't listen. You counted ribs, a xylophone of bones that lullabied you into sleep.

You heard *Beautiful*. From the six-ounce glass of tomato juice that stunned your tongue. From the fork you stabbed into lettuce leaves, from the cube of cheddar cheese that fueled your six-mile run along country roads. Whole rows of corn bowed down and whispered: *Beautiful*. The east-west swish of cars on Interstate 70: *Beautiful, beautiful, beautiful*.

Your world reduced to an equation of yes or no. No to the smear of chocolate frosting on cellophane, to chicken thighs frying, to glistening coins of pepperoni on a discarded slice. A storm of no, so much thunder and lightning. But yes to your hip bones sharpening the pockets of your size-five Levis, to the bathroom tiles cool white against your cheek. Yes to water when you withered and curled.

Nights, you bloomed under black lights, danced with your dwindling shadow. When the fat lady cut in, you knew to excuse yourself before she could crawl inside and live in you. In the bathroom, you leaned against the sink and whispered *Yes*. Afterward, you were clean again. Hollowed out and shouting.

SARAH FRELIGH is the author of *Sad Math*, winner of the 2014 Moon City Press Poetry Prize and the 2015 Whirling Prize from the University of Indianapolis. Among her awards are a 2009 poetry fellowship from the National Endowment for the Arts and a grant from the Constance Saltonstall Foundation in 2006.

58

PLUM JAM
FRANCES GAPPER

From our ladders we can see the plum-blue Malverns.
The army's bought up this harvest, still on the
trees. We pickers are a crew: boy scouts, gypsies,
PoWs, refugees, us girls in our mackintosh skirts
and hurden aprons. Blue for canning and bottling,
yellow to Ticklers jam factory in Grimsby. Tommies
eat plum, our Joe says. "What d'you want with eggs
and ham when you've got plum and apple jam?"
Sergeants get the raspberry, higher up the strawberry
and blackcurrant. We're feeding our boys, helping
the war effort. Lots goes to waste, though—fallen,
smashed, rotting where it lies.

FRANCES GAPPER'S story collections are *In the Wild Wood*
(2017), *The Tiny Key* (2009) and *Absent Kisses* (2002). Her
mini collection *Married to a Carrot* was a finalist for the
2017 Calvino Prize. Her flashes have been published in e.g.
The Cafe Irreal, Spelk, Meniscus, Ellipsis, Wigleaf and *Litro*.

THINGS LEFT AND FOUND BY THE SIDE OF THE ROAD

JO GATFORD

Baby car seats, sometimes with babies in them, swiftly recovered. Nettles flourishing in the face of toilet breaks. Things said in anger and in tiredness, whipped free from wound down windows. Singular shoes. Houses turned into islands, refusing to bow to the bypass, clinging to their land. Roadkill; fox-ochre and badger-stripe and innards turned outer. And crows, wherever things are dead and forgotten. Shopping lists never fulfilled. Plastic bags, flocks of them, as everlasting as the old gods. GPS-related swearing. A horse, filthy white, the same colour as its hay, watching the traffic, dreaming of leaping three lanes to greener grass. Dozing lorry drivers, longwave sewn into their sleep. The shouts of children: *Cows! Red car! Lions! Lions? No. Cows!* The snap-shut replies of parents who should have stopped for a wee miles ago. Imaginary friends, abandoned because of older sisters who said they were babyish. Garden centres where time is liminal and space folds in on itself somewhere between the box shrubs and the trellis. Petrol stations, though never when you need one. Yawns no longer suppressible. A cigarette butt flicked through a window slot, its glowing ash streaking back inside to burrow into denim thighs. Traffic cones like shells for urban hermit crabs, crushed and dented, flashing silently into the night. A moment of lapsed concentration. A time when you wouldn't make it home for Christmas, or the weekend, or at all. A time when these were Roman roads and the unexpected turn would not have existed. A time when all of this was nothing but fields. Car parts, tyre skids, blood spots, and perfect cubes of safety glass. The knowing sighs of EMTs. Roadside recovery phones standing at respectful intervals like neon orange sentinels. Angels, fallen, bewildered in concrete, wondering where all the souls have gone.

JO GATFORD is the co-founder of Writers' HQ, which means she is legitimately allowed to procrastinate about writing by writing about writing. Despite that, her novel *White Lies* was published by Legend Press in 2014 and her short fiction occasionally wins prizes. Much of it can be found at: www. jogatford.com

HE DIED WE LEFT HIM TIL MORNING

CHRISTOPHER GAUMER

We laid him down, 40 pounds of beagle. We took shovels; the earth opened easy like mouths for cheese.

Greg and Kathy stopped by to ask could they help. We were digging, the four of us.

Kathy sang *Amazing Grace*, which I hated, but what can you do?

Greg passed me Frank's body—solid and strange, only his ears still mobile, velvety smooth, like I imagine the space between dimensions.

Eventually dirt covered the body, covered the blanket, covered the hole, until it was just a plain flat spot of dirt that was, like it or not, our yard.

CHRISTOPHER GAUMER'S writing appears in *McSweeney's, The Rumpus, The Citron Review, Souvenir, Iodine Poetry Journal*, and elsewhere. Chris received his M.F.A. from Hamline University. He currently teaches at Randolph College where he is also the Assistant Director of the Randolph College M.F.A. program.

BECKY
BETH GILSTRAP

It's hard to think about the whitest of white girl
names. It's hard to think of playing post office with
you in the hall of our great grandmother's house.
Dirty planked floors. Biscuit dough in our hair—
yours tied up in tiger orange bows, mine cut short
because I'd used pinking shears to give myself a trim.
My monstrous teeth. All those times I fought kids
because they called me boy, which was the worst
thing back then, second only to Bugs Bunny. Grandpa
said I might as well get used to it. I'd never be the
delicate lace of your hem. But you and me, we wrote
letters on butterfly-shaped notepaper and summoned
cowboys to our rescue. Both of us were still olive-
skinned from summer, but sweater-wrapped and
giddy about stealing lipstick from the dollar store.
I stood six inches taller and my Lord, though we
were only a year apart, how the contrast knocked
me winded that day as you frosted your lips pink
and mine turned out to be a nothing kind of beige.
Your parents were still together, all of you living
swanky in a glass-heavy, high pitched 1980s something, honey. We played house and watched *Singing
in the Rain*. You swung on your canopy bed like

Gene Kelly and showed off your mirror, oval and bright in its stand. If someone had told me then, in between name-brand cheese crackers and Neapolitan ice cream, you would watch your daddy die on that same shag carpet, breathing your air into his lungs to no avail and some years later how you'd show up at Christmas with a baby you'd later abandon, how I'd write you a letter in prison about God and hope and playing, how I'd lose my faith not long after, I would've turned my jealousy into the shape of my hands on your cheeks, telling you I'm sorry. I'm so sorry. You were so fine in your patent leather and pageant gowns and all those backwards tumbles, the way your body flung itself and twisted, flung itself and pointed, flung itself—blooming tulle— and landed with high, sharp hands.

BONE WORDS
BETH GILSTRAP

The grass creases on his cheek when he rolled over kept me from waking him. A clump of clippings at his zygomatic bone. God knows what burrowing near his neck, near the occipital bone, along the base of his skull, where I'd held him. Soft spots no one thinks on. I like paying attention to places on a body most people take for granted. A smear of my lipstick (color, Medieval) true to its claim, everlasting on his Adam's apple—that sweet hunk of thyroid cartilage named for sin. His hair fallen across his eyes, still closed, still twitching like the horned beetle I'd picked off the dead pine next to our tent. I'd read in biology how when you see them, rarely anytime but dusk, they're only ever searching for their lovers or fighting—other males, only males, of course always fighting—for decaying fruit, or sap, favored mating grounds close to rotten wood. The sleeping boy is too sweet for fighting. He writes songs about my hair. The sleeping boy's brother will find out about us alone in the old growth, our chapped skin, our damaged tent, and helplessly hope our similar smells are his imagination gone dark. I found no female, but the beetle's hiss and mandible impressed me, a dribble of my own saliva as I pet his head, fighting the urge to tie a string around his dorsal plate and wear him as an amulet. Later, I will want to tell the sleeping boy's brother how lizards and snakes and beetles of the family *Lucanidae* have vast variations in size between juvenilia and adulthood, how their bodies are bound to environment with only a smidge of genetic influence, but all I can explain before he slams the door is how females have smaller, more powerful jaws. When I drive away, I will say "mandible" out loud to an empty car and roll all the windows down, praying for rain, praying for wings, praying for horns of my own.

BETH GILSTRAP is the author of *I Am Barbarella: Stories* (2015) from Twelve Winters Press and *No Man's Wild Laura* (2016) from Hyacinth Girl Press. She's Fiction Editor at *Little Fiction | Big Truths*. Her stories appear in *Ninth Letter*, *Wigleaf*, *Hot Metal Bridge*, and *Little Patuxent Review*, among others.

FRAGMENTS OF EVOLUTION
CAVIN GONZALEZ

Oxudercinae

A lot of creatures look like they're right in between step one and step two of the evolutionary process; like apes compared to man. The neatest example is the mudskipper. It's a lard of a creature with bulbous eyes plopped right on the top of its head. Imagine a fish transforming into a lizard; right before it sprouts legs, after it's developed lungs, that's the form of a mudskipper. I wonder for how many thousands of years those dingus fish flew out of the water and suffocated on the shores of an unknown world before the first of them possessed functioning lungs. How many millions of them died without ever knowing why they wanted to get onto land?

Crocodilians

There are swarms of alligators in Florida—banks of rivers piled with writhing monsters. Images don't do them justice. You have got to see them in person, in the wild, with their yellow eyes glaring at your limbs. In the space between your gaze and theirs exists only a carnivorous lust and a knowing, on their behalf, that you are nothing more than food. I wonder, when did the subconscious groupmind of their ancestors realize that they were indestructible? Camen. Crocodiles. Alligators. They've gone unchanged, for millions of years, without ever being choked out of the ecosystem.

Homo Sapien

Evolution is strange because we see billion-year long timelines that track the growth of legs and whatnot but sometimes it will occur instantaneously. One day you're a fish and the next you're a lizard. That's how it happened with my best friend. He was a kid. Then he was a man. It took no time at all. Like that—a synapse snapped in half and his curious playful tendencies evaporated and were replaced with the drive to sustain himself as best possible. He stopped skipping stones and started picking up shifts. One fertilized egg later and he evolved even further. It took five years for the entire metamorphosis to take place. Others refuse to evolve. Similar to lemmings, and their infatuation with plummeting off the side of cliffs, these beings were dedicated to extinction. While Darwin's finches were cracking the shells of nuts and hunting for insects these pitiful bastards were failing to carve out a niche in the modern food chain. They didn't breathe or suffocate, hunt or be hunted, they just fossilized behind gas stations and inside of cubicles.

CAVIN GONZALEZ is a twenty-two year old graduate from the University of Central Florida. He is the prose editor for *Soft Cartel* and book reviewer for *Pidgeon Holes*.

EMPIRE OF LIGHT
MELISSA GOODE

We walk side by side down a dark street, the houses dotted with windows of yellow light. A street lamp glows. Above us, the trees loom, bowing their heavy heads together, but above them the sky is blue, day-bright, spotted with white cumulus clouds. I stretch my hand to you and you take it, smiling. You are warm. I lift your hand and press it to my lips. "What time is it?" I say and you say, "Does it matter?" Maybe it is night—I am *so tired*. But there is all of that blue sky that makes me ache—it does not end. We could be going out or returning home. We could be lost. You are untroubled, calm. We wear the clothes we wore the night we met. We pass a house playing The Cure, "Close to Me"—the one where they are locked in a closet and clapping as they sink into the sea, the box filling with water. A couple dance in the window, ignoring the quick beat, they are dancing slow, so slow. A child squeals in another house, running down a wooden floor. It is not our daughter. Her pitch is different. The girl is laughing, as if she is being chased by someone she loves. You say, "We are almost there." A bird cries out. The air turns cold and smells of plants, damp earth, of upturning and settling. I kiss your hand again and it is not warm anymore. You walk faster now, as if you cannot wait to get there. You begin to run. I do not let go of you. We are rushing, racing, airborne and shot through with light. Our breathing is loud and fast. We are on the brink. We are a blip in time and space, nothing compared with matter and history, but that does not diminish a single thing about us.

I WANNA BE ADORED

MELISSA GOODE

You move closer towards me and you are not a
zombie or anything like that, although your face
is wrapped in grayish cloth. I don't know how
you aren't bumping into the furniture. I haven't
moved anything in our house, but still. You don't
walk unsteadily or hold out your hands to protect
yourself. It is 7pm. You could have just arrived home
from work and now walk towards me where I wait.
I wait. *How was your day?* No, let's not do that. I
won't ask you, and you won't ever fucking ask me.
Let's do this instead—I sing my favorite song and
you keep getting closer. I tell myself the mantra from
my therapist—*I have a feeling. I am not a feeling.* You
are so close now. Only two feet away. One foot. Your
breath is warm coming through the cloth and there
is the clean heat of your cologne. It is you. I grip
your upper arm—solid, hot, alive—if I could move
my hand, would I feel a pulse at your wrist? *I have
sadness. I am not sad.* "You love that fucking song,"
you say, and your voice is low, so low, scraping down
the inside of my veins. If I could speak, I would
say, "Talk, keep talking, scrape away at me." Or,
"Of course I still love that song. You know nothing

has changed, right?" *Nothing* and *Everything*. Stop. You lean down and I raise my face. Your height, my height—it is right. My stomach is somersaulting and I am breathing hard and all the rest of it. Like the first time (and yes, like the last, too, my beautiful). I feel the cloth already, although we have not yet kissed—the coarse weave, stiff, cotton, tight. And I can taste it—hospital, institutional, before it gets to you. The cloth does not bother me. I know the precise place where your mouth is, where it always was.

TONIGHT, WE ARE AWAKE
MELISSA GOODE

We were asleep when someone banged on our front door, with what? A wrench? It was deafening. It was a home invasion, except it wasn't. A fire fighter yelled at us to evacuate—there was a fire in the building next door.

You said, "Evacuate, really? Is that necessary?" He was already gone.

We walk down 15 flights of fire stairs and I am dizzy like I've been smacked over the head with a brick. Downstairs, in the front courtyard, we congregate in pajamas, bathrobes, slippers and flip-flops. Children clutch worn-out teddy bears. Some cry in their parents' arms, others are asleep again. The forbidden cats and dogs are here too.

The building next door billows black smoke into the orange, light-polluted sky. Our hair and clothes smell of smoke. Is it hotter? Someone says they see flames, but no one else does. Someone goes on and on about their asthma, dragging on their rescue inhaler, until they are taken away on a stretcher and silenced with oxygen.

You and I walk down the road to the 7-Eleven,

fluorescent-white and fridge-cold. We squint and shiver. Half of our neighbors are here, loitering in the doorway and in the aisles, reading their phones, licking Doritos-dusted fingers, sucking down Slurpees, flipping through Who, singing along to "She's Like the Wind" and "I Drove All Night" and every other fuck-I-love-this-song.

"Let's never go home!" someone yells to no one in particular.

We eat hot dogs even though we shouldn't. The bread is white, confectionary. We don't think about the meat—the pigs' ears, lips, assholes, whatever.

A few receive a text that we can return to the building. They, all of them, file out onto the street partway through "Constant Craving."

You buy us both large coffees and a packet of peanut M&M's. We sit at a table, hand in hand. We are still cold, but getting warmer. We are quiet. We will go home and fuck and not sleep at all tonight even though we have to work tomorrow. We will lie in our bed in the dark gray dawn and listen to the birds sing and swear it is the first time we have heard them.

MELISSA GOODE'S work has appeared in SmokeLong

Quarterly, Wigleaf, Forge Literary Magazine, Superstition Review and matchbook, among others. Her story "It falls" (*Jellyfish Review*) was chosen by Aimee Bender for *The Best Small Fictions 2018* (Braddock Avenue Books). She lives in Australia. You can find her here: www.melissagoode.com and twitter.com/melgoodewriter

FRAU ROENTGEN'S LEFT HAND

ANITA GOVEAS

The thumb is indistinct, mid-sized and slender. If it were a tree limb, it would reveal I was 50 years old. It can't sense I have 28 years before I die of intestinal cancer. It is doubtful the powerful rays had lasting impact. On me, not on history. But in the future, there will be more protections.

The forefinger contains the minerals that show the people who study these things that I was born in Zürich, lived in Vienna, ate well. But not yet. At this moment, the electrons exploding from the cathode ray tube show the outline, not the context. In the translucent flesh, there are other molecules lurking. Mine are only passed down through my beloved niece, who I adopted. There will be many kinds of invisible light.

The middle finger has the callus from writing that changed the shape of the top joint. All the odes I copied for my uncle, the poet. All the orders I recorded for my father, the cafe-owner. All the records I transcribed for my husband, the pioneer. All the letters I wrote for myself.

The fourth finger is dominated by the rings, the social contract. We met in my father's cafe, he was a gentleman. I never asked his hobbies. When he said to me "Anna, I need your help," I did so willingly. While I stood for an hour with my hand on the photographic plate, we discussed images and luminescence. It repelled me. It repelled me to be allowed to see what was usually revealed only by death.

The little finger holds the tiny mark from stabbing myself with a sewing needle. I always made my lace myself. I will make the dress I wear when Wilhelm is awarded the first Nobel prize, for this first x-ray we capture. The award for realising this exposure of my inner self will save lives.

The whole is surrounded by shadows of flesh and cloth. The granite-like bones could belong to my mother. They could belong to Queen Victoria. They could belong to Sarah Bernhardt.

The glow of this process brings out similarities, singularities. In the shadows, the wives of science provide tools and structure, but stay hidden.

LET'S SING EVERY SWEAR WORD WE KNOW

ANITA GOVEAS

You're a girl with a bell-shaped nose and an anchor-shaped birthmark. You're Antonia cos it's the closest to the only name your father picked out. You're not the reason he leaves, but you're not enough to make him stay. Your lungs are healthy when nothing else is, and you cry like the rushing river, all deadly undercurrents and no end. You only eat basmati rice and only wear shorts. You tattoo all your Barbies with indelible ink and sing all the swear words your babysitter teaches you in a chant that all the slaps in the world won't knock out. You're a girl with crescent-shaped teeth and your father's kidney-shaped earlobes. You wear grease like perfume and touch every slug. You love the way numbers line up in your head and hide in Maths lessons under your haphazard fringe and your Pearl Jam t-shirts. You're drawn to the smell of heated tarmac and leaves as brown as you under a magnifying glass. Your mouth says "fuck you" without you having to open it. You're a girl with grapefruit-shaped breasts and a water-melon bottom. You watch the boys as they watch you.

You don't have the words to make anyone stay, you talk to yourself when no one's listening. You leave as soon as you can and go back every weekend cos nobody else knows the words to your song.

ANITA GOVEAS is British-Asian, based in London, and fueled by strong coffee and paneer jalfrezi. She was most recently published in *JMWW, OkayDonkey* and *X-Ray lit.* She's on the editorial team at *Flashback Fiction*, an editor at *Mythic Picnic's* Twitter zine, a reader for *Bare Fiction* and tweets erratically @coffeeandpaneer

THE EXTINCTION MUSEUM: EXHIBIT #28 (INCANDESCENT BULB, UNLIT)

TINA MAY HALL

It used to be hard to tell manmade light from not. Satellites swam with the stars. Bulbs hidden behind glass mimicked the sky. In darkened rooms, we opened our eyes. Great washes of light played across the wall. Landscapes we'd never seen, giants with shellacked hair and painted lips. We were profligate with illumination. Some places never dimmed. We drowned the stars to cure our insomnia. Your grandfather took you outside on summer nights to watch the international space station zoom overhead, a meteorite, far-off vessel. You both imagined the people inside the metal case, floating like embryos, the carapace spreading its wings toward the sun. That summer, it flew over your yard again and again, binding the world with the thread of its orbit. When cut free, it spiralled out of our reach. After a few days we could no longer hear their voices, and after a few weeks, they were beyond our instruments of perception altogether, a reflection moving too fast.

I used to string fairy lights in every room, basked in their candle glow, never dreaming we'd be left only with flame. That the sparks of lightning bugs would bring us to tears. That every night would burn and burn and burn.

TINA MAY HALL lives in upstate New York. Her collection of stories, *The Physics of Imaginary Objects*, won the 2010 Drue Heinz Literature Prize. She is the recipient of an NEA grant, and her stories have appeared in *3rd Bed*, *Quarterly West*, *Black Warrior Review*, *The Collagist*, and other journals.

NOT THE WHOLE STORY

TONI HALLEEN

We did not get married because I was pregnant. I did not get the job. I do not know her name to this day. I did not need a storage unit. I do not know why I rented one. We cannot afford it. That is not true. It does not matter.

I do not understand how radio frequency works. I do not care. You may not make a super quick drawing for me. I should not eat wheat. That is not funny. I do not believe a word you are saying. Not on my watch. My voice does not sound like that.

Not everyone here is good looking. I will not come back. You are not on the list. That milk is not fresh. We are not getting along. You are not the love of my life. I will not stand for this. He does not know everything.

We do not have any more grapes. Do not touch me. I am not losing weight. That black and white movie you suggested was not any good. I do not read subtitles. I was not at home when it happened. Our plumber is not licensed, bonded or insured. I am not listening.

I am not responsible for all that stuff with Nancy

and her earaches. I am not hungry right now. They were not following instructions. I am not ready to let go. We did not get good advice. At least it's not the transmission. I could not handle that.

You have not apologized for any of the shit you put me through. I am not your mother. You have not paid me back that 45 dollars. I am not bluffing. That vase is not real and they knew it. That is not my problem.

TONI HALLEEN'S writing can be found in *Wigleaf, Gravel, Structo, WSQ*, the *StarTribune*, and elsewhere. In 2013, she won a Loft Literary Center Mentor Prize in fiction. Her play, *Soulless Bloodsucking Lawyers* won Best Musical at the Minneapolis Fringe Festival. Toni lives in Minnesota and is writing her first novel.

A BRIEF HISTORY OF TIME IN OUR HOUSE

STEVEN JOHN

This second is the same as the last, a press of the screen, the same exhalation. We lie in bed having social intercourse. Our hearts have pumped four ounces of blood.

Minutes replicate themselves like bacteria. Your quantum of likes leave you unloved. We have breathed sixteen litres of air. Little is different in this hour. Our livers have metabolised another drink, the sky sticks on black with white moon. Lunar and menstrual cycles are looping. With variant ingredients we cook the same suppers. Together we have shed a complete layer of skin.

We took an excursion around the sun again this year, five hundred million miles back to where we started. The Earth is a fraction warmer although it doesn't feel it here. Expended another 1.25% of our lives, give or take.

On the event horizon of a black hole, time is white. Our white blood cells die every day.

STEVEN JOHN lives in The Cotswolds UK where he writes short fiction and poetry. He's had work published in pamphlets and online magazines including *Riggwelter*, *Spelk Fiction*, *Fictive Dream*, *Cabinet of Heed* and *Ellipsis Zine*. Steven has won Bath Ad Hoc Fiction a record six times.

11:37

PETER KRUMBACH

She steps out of the bathroom dressed only in cards. Their values facing out, he can, even in the lowered light of her bedroom, clearly spot the pips, the swaying jacks, the 10 of diamonds that her thighs turn side to side as she struts along the bed. A fresh deck, can you smell? She reaches for him with one hand, the other holding a glass with two jokers drowned in gin. The window is open to the late-August heat. The pigeon on the sill bobs, then glides toward the tail-light lava eight floors below. It lands on the sidewalk, instantly drunk on the scent of burnt pistachios strewn by the feet of two laughing hustlers. One of them will, later that night, maim a man and not remember. The stoplight above them is alive, memorizing the miens of cabbies and cops, the drifting moods of ambulance howls. Beneath the awning glints a small blue stone in the lobe of a bicycle thief talking on his phone. Across the street the card man's wife leans against her car and smokes, her eyes trained on the high open window, its yellow so faint now, it is possible that what she sees isn't happening.

PETER KRUMBACH was born in Brno, Czechoslovakia. After graduating with a degree in visual arts, he left the country, and eventually found his way to the U.S. His writing has appeared in *The Adroit Journal, Copper Nickel, Michigan Quarterly Review, New Ohio Review* and elsewhere. He lives in California.

MISSING
MEGHAN LAMB

1

The Dead Woman in the Ditch is dead.

2

The Dead Woman in the Ditch was found—dead—in a ditch about 10 miles from the Small Town Where You Used to Live. The ditch is set between two different towns outside of it, and it belongs to none of them, is claimed by no one.

3

The Dead Woman in the Ditch is not a metaphor, an image, or an allegory for some other death.

She is a formerly-alive-formerly-real human, who was known by other people in the Small Town Where You Used to Live. She always said hello, says Ann Marie Rodriguez, of the mornings when they worked the same shift at the cannery. You used to drive along the road from which the cannery was visible each day, for work, but that was many years ago.

4

You've never gone back to the Small Town Where You Used to Live because it is inhabited by people who aren't going anywhere, who live in dingy houses with gray sunken roofs and thin lawns piled up with former toys and tools of no use.

5

The people of the Small Town Where You Used to Live claim that they're still investigating the death of the—now—Dead Woman in the Ditch. They claim the—now—Dead Woman in the Ditch has no near next of kin. They claim the—now—Dead Woman in the Ditch was missing for some time.

6

The Small Town Where You Used to Live is cold and poor, and no one there has very much, and no one there seems too surprised when things go missing. The Small Town Where You Used to Live once had two grand hotels, three movie theaters, but the buildings were torn down. I used to see her at Bill's Tavern, says Kathleen Prevonka, speaking for the place everyone there still knows and recognizes well. You try to picture it, a dark room filled with damp smells and wood paneling, a dart board, and a back room filled with smoke.

7

You've never gone back to the Small Town Where You Used to Live. This time of year, the hills would all be thick with snow, completing the effect of sinking downward, sinking inward, sinking very deep.

8

The—now—Dead Woman in the Ditch was never going anywhere.

MEGHAN LAMB is the author of *All Your Most Private Places* (Spork Press, 2019) and *Silk Flowers* (Birds of Lace, 2017). Her work has appeared in *Quarterly West*, *DIAGRAM*, and *Redivider*, among other publications. She currently serves as the nonfiction co-editor of *Nat. Brut*, a journal of art and literature dedicated to advancing inclusivity in all creative fields

KANEKALON

RAVEN LEILANI

A Beauty Supply's yellow mouth opens in far out lavender Queens, and I have a new synthetic ponytail. I secure the hair with a drawstring and thrash, imagine a man's hand, reaching for it like a doorbell. The ponytail looks like what it costs. Which is to say, sometimes a girl wants to look in the mirror and see that soggy dollar off-brand loll that is catnip to dumb, beautiful men, that barcode on the base of her neck saying, wholesale. I degrade myself before I leave the house so the men I meet have to come up with something else to do. In the movies, sometimes a girl tumbles into a man and promptly slides her neck underneath his foot. Which is to say, sometimes a meet-cute is just a dude shopping for furniture, and the girl has pie eyes, an overinvestment in the flailings of mediocre men, and does not realize she is a chair. So there is no spontaneity. Just furious arithmetic, reclining at the bar, legs apart. So I get a beer and I'm closing in, and he thinks he's closing in on me. I'm jealous of his certainty, wondering what happens between boy and man that drafts a suite of absolutes, this *what you need to understand is,* this *actually.* Some parts of this still need work. I flip my ponytail over my shoulder and get it in my mouth, for a moment look like what I am. Which is to say, sometimes I go home and eat six donuts. Sometimes I yell out of the window, looking for something with a heartbeat to throttle between my thighs. But it doesn't have to be perfect. It is enough to be young and willing. It is enough to look into his eyes and intimate I am half woman, half child, tackle on a silver line, fat, preening cherry and liquid spine. Which is to say, the ecstasy of powerlessness, when I lean in and pretend the only word I know is yes.

RAVEN LEILANI'S work has appeared in *Granta, New England Review, Split Lip Magazine* and *Smokelong Quarterly*. Work is forthcoming in *McSweeney's* and *Conjunctions*. She is the fiction editor at *Ruminate Magazine*, and an MFA candidate at NYU.

SELF PORTRAIT WITH EARLY DECEMBER

PAIGE LELAND

Houston is raining, has been since August, and my father calls to tell me it's snowing up north, but, I say, *at least snow doesn't flood*, at least there's a soft place to fall. My room is somehow smaller now and there is nobody here to hold me. But what is holding but twisted limbs that stretch until they break? Everyone that has ever claimed to love me has left. The last few nights I have been waking up at 3am to shadows of bodies that no longer exist, handprints half embossed in the sheets. When I let myself dream, you are a cartoon—a blond boy driving that CRV with his knee propping up the wheel and when I wake up I'm smiling but not because I miss your arms, or because I wish you were cradling me, but because nothing was ever easier than those nights, that shaking transmission, the air that clung to the backs of our necks. I have left myself a thousand miles away in the last place you kissed me, hands twisted but still reaching.

PAIGE LELAND is a native of Mid-Michigan finding her way in Houston, Texas. A 2017 Pushcart Prize nominee, her work has appeared in *Glass Mountain*, *The Tahoma Literary Review*, formercactus and elsewhere. She currently works in advertising and spends her free time with her boyfriend and two cats.

A WARM MOTHERLY LOOK

ROBERT LOPEZ

My sister smothered the baby to keep it quiet because everyone had paid good money to hear the guest speaker. What I'm saying is it was not premeditated or malicious. Now, it is true that it wasn't my sister's baby. My sister doesn't have any children herself, but does have a warm and motherly look about her. One assumes this is why she was entrusted with the baby once the lecture began. It's also true we don't know who the parents were or how the baby came to be in the lecture hall. Some speculated it was the guest speaker's baby and this could well be true. The guest speaker seemed upset when my sister smothered the baby, though it was for her own benefit and of those in her audience. I was there to do the sound and lights, which had been my job for the last two years. As for my sister, I know she'd love to be a mother, but is old-fashioned and reluctant to have a child out of wedlock.

ROBERT LOPEZ is the author of three novels, *Part of the World*, *Kamby Bolongo Mean River*, and *All Back Full*; and two story collections, *Asunder* and *Good People*. www.robertlopez.net

BREATHLESS

PAUL LUIKART

I try to make amends with Breathless, a stripper I know whose real name is Anna. I used to go to her club. We got drunk all the time and fooled around a lot. I told her once I'd marry her. Anyway, she meets me at Julio's, a new little spot where I've been spending my time. It has coffee and all variants of coffee, plus brunch-y food like fried eggs with sprouts on top. Breathless glances around and says, "Wow, Mr. Fancy."

"It's because I can't be in the club anymore," I say. "Can I read this to you?"

"What is it?" she says.

"My little mea culpa. Remember? I'm trying to tell you I'm sorry."

"Fine."

"I wrote it all down. You can keep it if you want. After I read it to you."

"Fine."

So I start reading. I make it through, "I regret that I manipulated your feelings and—" before Breathless laughs and stands up, mouths, "Fuck off," and walks out. Her thick heels pound the wooden floor and she shoves the door out of her way. I watch for a couple minutes, waiting for her to come back. But she's never coming back. Okay.

I take out my phone to call my sponsor but check my email instead. There is, of course, nothing new. In moments of clarity, such as they are, I understand that what I really want is a note from the people of Earth. "Hello and welcome back. You can still count yourself among our billions."

PAUL LUIKART is the author of the short story collections *Animal Heart* (Hyperborea Publishing, 2016) and *Brief Instructions* (Ghostbird Press, 2017.) He is an adjunct professor of fiction writing at Covenant College in Lookout Mountain, Georgia. He and his family live in Chattanooga, Tennessee.

SIREN

FIONA J. MACKINTOSH

In the wet slap of the haar, the lassies slit the herring mouth to tail and pack them into briny barrels. I see her head move among the rest, brown curls escaping from her shawl. She has the juice of silver fishes in her veins—it's in the raised blue of her wrists, her raw fingers, in the taste of oysters when I lick her down below, her skirt canted up and knees apart.

They say despair can be a man's making, but that's not how it feels to me. I give her everything I have— primrose plants, stockings, greenhouse fruits— and everything I am, a stiff-collared man behind a counter at the bank. She says my palms smell of money and loves their smoothness on her skin, but then she sees the brown sails coming, the lads home from the draves, swaggering in their thigh-high boots. She rests her elbows on the bar, pink mouth open, as this one tells of breaching humpbacks and that one tells of waves the height of mountains. I loathe their muckled arms and sunburnt faces and wish them at the bottom of the sea.

She knows the only times I venture out are on the calmest days, sometimes to cast a line and once a year to watch the puffins hatch. It's not an epic life, not one likely to inspire the poets. But when the *Reaper* goes down with all hands lost, it's my door she comes to and cleaves herself to me from head to heel. She says, "I need a man who willnae leave me wantin'." Afterwards, cross-legged on the bed, she hangs a pair of cherries over her ear and, giddy with my unexpected luck, I take them in my mouth, stones and all.

THE CHEMISTRY OF LIVING THINGS

FIONA J. MACKINTOSH

The blue ones make me dream of thistles, make me loop-de-loopy, shaking bubbles from my wrists. The big yellow ones are slow-witted and tip me into drenching sleep at unexpected hours. The white diamonds have a certain easy charm, but it's the tiny silver ones I like the best. In my cupped palm they roll like mercury balls, but in my head they fizz and dazzle, splintering into gaudy reds and greens. They're the reason I can glide above the broken glass, put a soft hand on my husband's shoulder as he tells our guests another story and nods to me to bring the coffee and dessert. Smoke coils beneath the lamp, softening the light. The faces round the table seem familiar, but I don't know who they are, the men with bristled hair, the women oiled and shiny with cat's-eye glasses and wet teeth. Mouths open, voices bourbon-loud with the looseness of late evening. The noise pulls close around my head like curtains as I rinse the dirty plates and spear a perfect sprig of mint in every peach sorbet. Against the back-splash, the pill bottles gleam, and I promise-touch each one for later. You and you and you. Through the window, just beyond the house-thrown light, a young deer stares at me with deep, black eyes. I see its dappled hide, a white stripe on its haunch that may or may not be a scar. I know at once it's come to lure me out into the dark and unfamiliar, onto bleak, untrodden ground. I press my hands five-fingered on the window, and, when I wipe away the cloud my breath has made, the deer has gone like it was never there at all.

FIONA J. MACKINTOSH is a Scottish-American writer living near Washington D.C. In 2018, she won the Fish Flash Fiction Prize, the NFFD Micro Competition, the October Bath Flash Award, and *Reflex Fiction's* autumn contest. Her short stories have been listed for the Bristol, Galley Beggar, and Exeter Prizes.

AN INHERITANCE
LUTIVINI MAJANJA

The three girls make an excellent exhibit even before they are photographed. Their forward march drowns out the catcalls and the "Check your weight!" calls. Three girls in dresses and shoes not quite identical. Shades of purple. They are unfazed from the trip that started with them chasing after the bus that threatened to leave them even though they had been patient, waiting for the next available ride.

Their shoulders move freely as if they hadn't flinched when the bus conductor nudged their backs as he pushed them, into the vehicle—'Harakisha!'—and then whispering the unsayable to the eldest of them. She is 19. The youngest one heard it too. Eight years old, she didn't understand. The 14-year-old will not dwell on the fact that the conductor's long fingernail tickled her palm, a provocation, when she gave him the fare, and again when he returned the change.

With their various going-somewhere faces they reflect back the sunshine, moving to a beat— their own. Arms swing, claiming all the space that can be claimed on the crowded footpaths. They set aside how frightened they felt when they had to also jump out of the moving vehicle that wouldn't stop at the bus stop, not even for the youngest one. In their finest wear, they are going to the studio to get photographed for their mother. She wants to remember them innocent.

LUTIVINI MAJANJA lives in Nairobi, Kenya. Her writing has been published in *Flash Frontier*, *Popula*, *The Elephant*, *Kikwetu*, *New Orleans Review*, *Kwani?*, *McSweeney's* and *The Golden Key*. She has an MFA in Creative Writing from the University of Maryland, College Park.

LESSONS FROM MY MOTHER

PROSPER MAKARA

I'm sitting on the floor as my mother plaits my hair.

I always think of myself as a canvas, my mother the painter.

"You should be grateful that he wants to marry you." My mother paints in light paint, her strokes very soft. Almost imaginary.

"Never stop opening your legs like a well-oiled door even if you don't want to."

She divides my thick hair with a comb.

"Nurse his fragile ego by thanking him for pounding you. It doesn't matter if you are hurt or not sated." She intones in a desperate voice, plaiting feverishly and yet, in a surprisingly soft manner.

"We were born to submit to our men."

She yanks my hair; taken aback by the momentary surge of pain I yelp.

"Women are meant to endure the pain."

I think of my father's fists pummelling into her flesh in a kindness reminiscent of enemies. My buttocks become itchy. The floor is very cold.

"We can never run away from our culture."

This time her work-gnarled hands swiftly paint in a darker hue. Her strokes not so gentle. She, my mother, is a passionate painter.

In the moment before the paint dries I wonder what kind of culture prepares women to die.

I think of Ryan with his long tapering fingers, fingers which speak of a gentleness not common in men.

Will he pummel me that hard?

If he does, I will use those fingers as confetti at my other wedding.

PROSPER MAKARA is a Biotechnology Undergraduate Student at the Chinhoyi University of Technology in Zimbabwe. Though fond of science, Prosper is equally passionate about literature and draws his inspiration from Chimamanda Adichie and Warsan Shire.

LOOP-THE-LOOP

DAN MALAKOFF

At Basic, a gunship catches your eye. It swoops, your wife rounding toward the bed.

"Anyone home, recruit?"

When did she first take you to bed? The headboard drums voodoo on the wall. On the dresser, a framed photo falls onto its back. You huff wet words in her ear. Kate, Kate. She moans, moans, ahhhs.

"Wake the fuck up, soldier."

The gunship glides into the path of the sun. When you can see again, you see your drill sergeant inches from your face. Don't explain that even rotors Katekatekate-ing bring her to mind. That you love her too much.

"Is your brain a fucking bag of shit?"

* * *

Kate, in bold print on the divorce papers. In your basement efficiency, home from tour number two, you and your empty aquarium which can't support fish. "Feel guilty, bitch," comes out. Then, "No, no," as you bite down hard on your forearm. You fall back into the couch. You say, "Kate, Kate, Kate," and can't see the Apache through the sand its rotors kick up. Bootprints like your own left in the dunes to lead you snaking. The haze splits open. A woman in hijab. Eyes, skin, no lower jaw. Blown clear off. You punch your head to stop it.

Breathe, the PsyD tells you every Tuesday and Thursday. "It's a sort of infatuation," he explains. "Just the mind fixating, doubling back."

You wish he would stop saying *trigger*.

DAN MALAKOFF'S stories have appeared in *Pleiades*, *River Styx*, *Wigleaf*, *Southern Humanities Review*, and other journals. His novella, "Steel City Cold," was published by Comet Press. He holds an MFA from the University of Pittsburgh and lives in Pittsburgh.

BOOM
MICHAEL MARTONE

Serious mining of the natural gas reservoir, a reserve that would become known as the Trenton Field in east central Indiana, began in the late 1880s. Overnight, thousands of wells were drilled. The deposits of fossil fuel in the huge interconnected field spread over 5,000 square miles, nearly the size of the state of Connecticut, contained a trillion cubic feet of gas and a billion barrels of oil. To prove that the gas was flowing from the new well bores, the operators tapped the mainline, piping off a portion of the flow to set the surplus spectacularly ablaze. The flames towered over the plains and prairies, forests of fire. The flares could be seen as far north as Fort Wayne. And the light over the horizon above Indianapolis roiled and flickered, a manmade display of the *Aurora borealis*. These constantly combusting gas flares came to be known as *"Flambeau."* The discovery led to an industrial boom for commerce, illumination, manufacturing, especially of glass products. Ball Brothers, Henry, Hoosier, Root, and Sneath—all these companies were attracted by the cheap and seemingly inexhaustible fuel. Art Smith, The Bird Boy of Fort Wayne, began his flying career just as the great gas field of Indiana was reaching its peak. Aloft, even in daylight, he could see over the horizon, south to the far reaches of Delaware, Jay, Blackford, and Grant Counties and the copses of yellow orange flames flaring in the distance, the light seemingly floating, like oil on the shimmering melting azure of liquefied air. At night, the *Flambeau* burning created a deep blue mirage, a blanket that wavered like waves on a black sand shore. In 1912, the Chamber of Commerce of Gas City hired Smith to celebrate The Boom by writing BOOM over the booming city ringed with flaming groves and arbors of *Flambeau* whose jets of combusting gases leapt up toward Smith's vapory writerly combustion, fingers pointing, twitching flickering hands grasping the slowly expanding, ever thinning rings of the mute BOOM.

KLAUS WEBER, CURB HOUSE NUMBERER

MICHAEL MARTONE

Around here there are no blocks as such, just cul-de-sacs and circles and dead ends and half streets and alleys. The numbers make no sense. And some of the numbers have fractions and some have letters attached as an afterthought and some have all three—numbers and fractions and letters. And the letters are upper case and lower case. The lady who lives in 2A is all the time taking mail over to 29 and vice versa. The mail trucks wander around looking for the number that might be a number. There's no rhyme or reason to it. I do use stencils so most of the job is taping the cutout paper to the curb. Then I just fill up the spaces with the aluminum paint. It glows in the light. When I finish there is this sparkling drift stuck in the gutter. And then I move on to the next house leaving the last one's number to dry. Often I am just guessing at the next number. It makes no sense as I said. Later, much later, I return to peel the stencils from the curb. Sitting there in the gutter I can't help myself. I do some weeding along the edges of the anonymous lawns. Ground mint and multi-flora rose and mimosa and crab grass. Weeds look like weeds. And they are everywhere.

MICHAEL MARTONE'S new books are *Brooding* and *The Moon Over Wapakoneta*. He lives in Tuscaloosa, below the Bug Line.

from KYSO FLASH

YOU CAN FIND JOY IN DOING LAUNDRY

KATHLEEN MCGOOKEY

Laundry is loyal. Laundry always waits, unlike a hungry friend or a French lover. Laundry needs you like a floor needs a mop. It's not just work, it's joy, available for the taking. Lucky you. Nothing smells like a fresh start like a load of whites, tossed in at 3am after a child threw up, a woeful stuffed lamb tumbling dizzily among the sheets. If bleach doesn't work, try baking soda. Try Cascade mixed with a half cup of Dawn. Remember to blot and never scrub. Blood, chocolate, and glue usually never leave you, constant as weather, but other stains grow pale, then drift off like ghosts to gaze at the clouds. And though their presence bothered you at first, you forget them so easily, like stray thoughts, like that boy who smelled of mint and his mother's detergent sitting next to you in 10th grade biology, who held your hand at the movies, once. He had black hair and long eyelashes and fingernails bitten to the quick. What was his name?

KATHLEEN MCGOOKEY'S most recent book is *Heart in a Jar.* Another book is forthcoming from Press 53 this year. Her work has appeared in *Crazyhorse, December, Field, Glassworks, Ploughshares, Prairie Schooner,* and *Quarterly West.* She has received grants from the French Ministry of Foreign Affairs and the Sustainable Arts Foundation.

A ROMAN ROAD

ADAM McOMBER

They come from Rome, the revelers, all gold and violet tattered. They come in carts and broken litters, sedans and palanquins. They ride on bridled mules and once-fine horses. They walk and limp and drink a bitter wine. They remember (however vaguely) a prior age, a higher light: plumed gardens full of olive trees, a villa strung with burning lamps. They remember halls of fine marble, the lips of pale young men. They sing and bare their teeth and move their strange procession along the dusty road. Some wear masks of ivory, some of hammered silver, others still are bare-faced. One of them, a tall man with long arms, carries a horn. He uses it to make a reedy sound. Another strums a broken harp. And still another pounds a clay urn as if it were a drum. The sky is vague and white. The trees, dead and leafless. The revelers do not pause to look at the ruins on the outskirts of their city. They know the ruins well enough. Fallen aqueducts and shattered tombs, rose-colored brickwork, all in pieces and silvered over with lichen. Here in the countryside, the hills are brown and burned. And the autumn wind seems to bear a message: *take comfort, men, for all is dying, all will soon be dead.* But these revelers, they do not pause, they do not listen. They make their way deeper into the country, moving toward the valley of the Tiber. They know their destination well enough: the storied pleasure dome, the labyrinth and the feasting hall. The country house where Roman men have always come when they are in need of delight. These revelers remember their fathers going to such a place. They've heard stories all their lives. And now they too want to drink the house's wine and eat its fabled dish, the stewed tongues of songbirds. They want to lay in dark chambers and stroke the house's handsome ghosts (the limber soldiers and the athletes and the dark-eyed youths who once lounged on the steps of the Forum). These men, the final revelers, they want this country palace, this dream. The Huns and Vandals will not harm them there. Falling will not harm them. They remember, as they walk together, what their fathers called this place: *my house of gray forgetting. My spilling forth. My dust.*

ADAM MCOMBER is the author of two short story collections, *This New And Poisonous Air* and *My House Gathers Desires* (BOA Editions) as well as a novel, *The White Forest* (Touchstone). His work has appeared recently in *Conjunctions*, *Diagram* and *Fairy Tale Review*. He lives in Los Angeles and teaches at Vermont College of Fine Arts.

A POST-TRAUMATIC GOD
HEATHER MCQUILLAN

Tāwhirimateā tried to stand his ground but was outnumbered. The ground he stood on was his mother's unstable belly, doughy and stretched from so many sons. She let him down in the end, as all mothers do. Let go of his hand. This he remembers: darkness humid with sweat and the sourness of spilt milk, the hau, the beat, the pulse, pressed tight between his parent's renditions of love, their keening drone, beneath the shouting of his brothers and the TV turned up too loud. This he remembers: the rupture, the coming into the blue lights and sirens and the whero of eyelid blood when he closes them against the glare. His mother convulsing, his father gone, brothers scattered. This he remembers: a stranger's hand on his shoulder. The weightlessness of feet that have nowhere to stand. The weight of swallowed words deep in his belly while they click Bic pens. In resting he is jolted. Thought spirals into cyclone cones—always back to the eye of the storm. He's tried the recommended doses but they don't work for him so he pulls sharply from the bed he shares with a thin-boned woman, takes his clenched fists away from her frail flesh and he runs. His feet tread heavy along his mother's backbone, along the length of the coastline out to the headland, where he howls at a cloud-blacked father-sky and slaps his chest until the skin burns. This he knows: cold air and the taste of blood in his throat and the Tāwhiri sits on the paint-peeled seat outside the takeaway shop. He is waiting for the skinny woman to fetch him back in her beat-up car. Sweat stains the curves of his white singlet. His father is hazy today. His mother has not rumbled for some time. His brothers are pencilled scars on the horizon.

HEATHER MCQUILLAN is Director for The School for Young Writers in New Zealand. Awards include the Australian CAL Best Prose Prize 2018, Best Small Fictions 2017 and winner of both the NZ Flash Fiction Day and Micro Madness competitions 2016. Heather is an award-winning writer of novels for young readers.

IT'S SHAPED LIKE A GRIN, THEY SAY

K.C. MEAD-BREWER

There's a crooked bridge where all the kiddies go to jump. It isn't about death or the moon or the pines that keep crowding in and crowding in, their black night robes making them look like pointed witches' hats. It isn't about the parents who've said their prayers and drunk their drinks and hit or kissed or both their kids. It's about that crooked bridge and the hard-eyed water beneath it. Sweet Uncle Steve said it's where we all go down to drink. It's where we drag back our collective inspiration, our ghosts our dreams our boogeymen, The Dark Man, The Shadow Man, The Man in the Hat Standing at the Foot of Your Bed. You look down into that big glassy face, The Water, and you see the rabbits going tharn, scarecrows shambling off their crosses, lagoon monsters waving webbed hands and fluttering slimy gills, all the monsters flashing past you, headlights on a highway. And who can say no to that? Even if it spooks you. Your hands are already sweaty on the bars, the support beam, that last inch of rope. You're all alone when you're on the crooked bridge, even if a party drove you to it. Your girlfriend, your boyfriend, they just got their license, their new car, and oh, it smells good, don't it? Squeaking leather, cold windows, knuckles flexing on the wheel. Even if you all come together, holding hands, a sacred promise, your fingers cut and bleeding into each other, maybe you did it sitting around a campfire, maybe the smoke's still pinkening your eyes. But the crooked bridge knows you, it gets you alone. It has corners, the crooked bridge, and dips. You won't leave without looking away lost into that water, the kind that stretches down deeper and deeper as if the bottom were a slingshot pulling back and pulling back and you can't look away because when it finally snaps forward to hit you—Oh, that big black eye. The Water. The water that opens up its arms to you, grabbing, drawing, a hug, a hand around your ankle, and says, Come on home, baby. Come on home.

K.C. MEAD-BREWER lives in Baltimore, Maryland. Her writing appears in *Electric Literature*, *Carve Magazine*, *Strange Horizons*, and elsewhere. She is a graduate of the 2018 *Clarion* Science Fiction & Fantasy Writers' Workshop and of *Tin House's* 2018 Winter Workshop. For more information, visit kcmeadbrewer.com and follow her @meadwriter.

NIÑOS DE LA TIERRA
JOSÉ ENRIQUE MEDINA

I grew up believing there were children under the earth.

"When it rains, they come out," Abuelita said, wrapped in the exoskeleton of her black rebozo. "One sting, and you're dead."

After a storm, my little brothers and I guarded the windows with plastic swords, watching mud shining in moonlight.

"They're bald like a new-born," Abuela whispered with her mothball breath. "They cry like a child."

We listened, between wind's pauses, for their wail.

If we broke a plate, she frowned, her face wrinkled like caterpillar-skin.

"They have six legs and little baby fingers at the end of each leg. They kidnap bad kids."

We hid, blankets curled around us like cocoons.

Covered in church veil cobwebs, she slammed her hand against the door. We huddled together. "Don't go outside. The children of the earth are going to get you."

"What are they?" we asked.

"They're Satan's children. Part baby, part tiger."

One day, I flipped her the middle finger.

"I'm going to grab that little finger and twist it and give it to the earth babies." She grimaced. "They'll drag you to hell."

When Abuelita died, we put dead cockroaches in one of her shoeboxes, and buried it in the garden. We sealed her grave with water we said was holy, trapping her underground.

All that summer we ran on top of her, laughing, surrounded by swollen roses.

JOSÉ ENRIQUE MEDINA earned his BA in English from Cornell University. He writes poems, short stories and novels. His work has appeared in *Tahoma Literary Review*, *The Burnside Review*, *Pretty Owl Poetry*, and other publications. When he is not writing, he enjoys playing with his baby chicks, bunnies and piglets on his farm in Whittier, California.

THIS WEEKEND
TRACY LYNNE OLIVER

My mom will crawl into my lap like a baby and I will let her. My mom's legs are so long and heavy with block feet. She walks with a jolting stiffness. My mom's legs are Frankenstein but I will still hold her. There. In my lap. I will ask her to nuzzle me and to paw my breasts through my shirt, making gross grunting bird noises. My mom will be as drunk as I will be. This weekend. Come with us. I plan to get nosebleeds. If the nosebleeds don't happen spontaneously I will find ways to make them happen. I won't carry napkins. I want to be waried by strangers. I will bring many extra shirts. This weekend. You can punch me. Meet me there. It's the place that's too hot for the horses. I've seen how the sun kills them. The saddest thing is a dying horse. That time I hit one with my car. How I sat beside it while it died. Begging it to rise again, let me on its back, how we could just ride away and eat grass and lick salt. If he would just get up. Those last breaths kicked up dust. This weekend, if you join us, you can try to stop me from peeling the skin from my fingers. These odd spots that itch. Finger-colored nubs that grow and disappear randomly like twitching brown cock-humps out of gopher holes. I can't stop them from feeling victorious whenever I scratch them. They make me look foolish. I've tried to pinch them off but they just come back. Now I'm digging and peeling. This weekend, help me find their roots. This weekend, if you come, you can wrap the bandages around my right hand because I am right-handed and the left-wrapped bandages will be too loose to do any good. The skin is red and smooth. It looks lit from behind. This weekend with my mom and my nose blood and my fleshless fingers and your helpful bandaging and all the alive horses, indoors, where it is cool. We could be there together. Drinking vodka in the smoke.

TRACY LYNNE OLIVER is attempting to make a new name for herself in this writing game. Check out her cool website: tracylynneoliver.com or just follow her on Twitter @T_L_OLIVER

FIRE

BRENDA PEYNADO

When I was eight years old, I watched a fire leap over the forest in glowing arcs and the men in my family battle it away. The fire had taken out farms on the panhandle for a hundred miles each way, from Tallahassee to Pensacola. I had just been put down for bedtime after the family's Sunday dinner when my uncle shook me out of bed and told me, *Go fetch the buckets, girl.*

I ran up to where I could see a glow like orange dawn over the hilltop. The heat almost burned my face off. The fire whizzed from tree to tree in arcs like deadly rainbows. The men passed buckets up the tree line. They were soaking the trees on the border of the farm in violent crashes of foaming water against bark. Trees exploded from boiling sap with deep popping sounds like drums pulling themselves open. I saw one come apart right in front of me, the sap glimmering as it burst, like amber that couldn't take its own history. I, useless with my fistfuls of empty buckets, froze at the top of the hill. I felt like something inside of me was ready to explode. I wanted to stand there until those arcs burned me with the trees. I stared, with the heat on my face, until my father finally screamed at me from the bucket line to *move*. But we were dwarfed against those loud, raging arches, and eventually the water planes got there with their rain.

While we cleared all the underbrush away, my cousin whispered, *I saw you, up there not doing anything.* I wacked him with my bucket and then he grabbed my hair and held me down in the hot mud. *You're just a girl*, he said.

I'm not a girl, I yelled, full of rage and flailing. I pushed him off and ran.

He caught up with me and grabbed my shirt by the fistful and the buttons tore, and he said, *Look, you are a girl*, as if that settled everything and we could never again be friends.

When I walked back home through the crackling woods, I left my shirt open to show what he'd done, to show the sap burning inside, to show how ready I was to burst, to turn others to ash, the word girl meaning *fire*.

BRENDA PEYNADO'S stories have won an O. Henry Prize, a Pushcart Prize, the *Chicago Tribune's* Nelson Algren Award, a Fulbright Grant to the Dominican Republic, and other prizes. Her work appears in journals such as *The Georgia Review*, *The Sun*, *The Southern Review*, *The Kenyon Review Online*, and *The Threepenny Review*. She currently teaches in the MFA program at the University of Central Florida.

AFTER THE FLOOD WATERS CAME
DOMINICA PHETTEPLACE

After the flood waters came, the sharks swam into town. You could see the sharp edges of their dorsal fins cutting the surface, passing by stop signs. Most were smaller than the kayak I paddled around in, but some were bigger and the largest one swam right underneath me. It was beautiful in a way that only something terrifying could be.

The first day of the flood was the best one. The water was clear and you could imagine it was somehow cleansing, that it could somehow absorb the sins of the town. The second day and after, the water grew cloudy and filmy, as it began to dissolve the grime off the streets and poison from the factories. This was sin absorbed and it was sin retained and there was no looking away from it, even if you closed your eyes, the smell still got in. You could still see sharks, but now only their fins, not their bodies.

Once the water lost its clarity it was time to abandon other hopes. The hope that I could paddle around town forever, never worrying about my dwindling supply of bottled water and candy bars. The hope that whales and sea turtles would follow the sharks in and the hope that coral reefs would establish themselves on the pothole-ridden streets that cars used to drive on. The hope that a fertile world could spring from our mistakes and ruin. That we could be delivered, that we could be rescued, that we could get better.

DOMINICA PHETTEPLACE is a math tutor who writes literary and science fiction. Her work has appeared in *Analog*, *Asimov's*, *F&SF*, *Zyzzyva*, *Ecotone*, *The Pushcart Prize Anthology* and *The Year's Best Science Fiction and Fantasy*.

ABSTINENCE ONLY

MEGHAN PHILLIPS

After the girls left, the school started to stink. The fug of boy bodies. Old onions and sprouted garlic, a weeks-old Arby's beef and cheese, dirty socks and cum-crusted gym shorts. The girls were all sweet mint gum and cherry blossom hand lotion. Sun-warmed laundry fresh. Shampoo like the ice cream case at the farm show—creamsicle, black raspberry, cake batter, cherry vanilla. After the girls left, the health teacher's warnings took on new meaning. Abstinence was the only way to protect yourself, the only way to really be safe. We thought the girls were playing with us. Some new coy shit to get us hard enough to rent limos for prom. To surrender letter jackets and chess tournament pins. To make it Facebook official. No fooling around in the percussion closet in the band room before school or soft hands down our waistbands or tongue-sucking, lip-mashing in the parking lot after school. No signs on game day, "Go #14" with a big heart. No texts—*I <3 u, bb*. After the girls stopped touching licking holding loving us, we were so lost in our sweaty-fisted longing we hardly noticed the girl-shaped gaps in our days. The empty chairs at quiz bowl, at debate, in choir, at lunch. The field hockey field, all unmarked turf. The softball diamond, chalk lines pristine. The stacks of papers passed to the front of the room were half as thick as they once were. Stuck in an endless wet dream, we didn't know on that last day when the teachers had finally had it with no homework, no essays, blank test papers and closed mouths, when they told Allie and Fatima and Bethanne and Liz and Rebecca and Shantae to take their chairs to the hall and sit until they were ready to participate, that the last thing we'd hear from the girls was the scrape of metal legs on asbestos tile. That the last thing we'd see of them was their chairs piled high on the school's front lawn, like branches waiting for a bonfire.

FINAL GIRL SLUMBER PARTY

MEGHAN PHILLIPS

We don't braid each other's hair. Can't stand the yank tug of the brush, the drag of bristles over scalp. Warm breath on the backs of our necks. We sit knee-to-knee. Rub each other's scars with cocoa butter. Pink arms pink thighs pink cheeks seamed through like C-minus home ec. projects.

No one is left alone. Not to go to the kitchen for a diet soda. Not even to use the bathroom. We all use the downstairs powder room and pee with the door cracked.

We can't watch romantic comedies now. A man follows a girl to her office, to her favorite coffee shop, to her childhood bedroom. He finds out her favorite flower. Blasts her favorite song from a boombox on her lawn. We know what that is. It's not love.

None of us want to play Fuck, Marry, Kill anymore. Pretty sure not fucking's the reason we're still here. Pretty sure fucking's just another kind of stabbing, another way to get us out of our skin. Pretty sure all the boys we'd want to fuck are dead anyways. None of us can imagine being married. We don't have to imagine who we'd kill.

We greet the pizza boy with kitchen knives and hatchets and baseball bats one-handed behind our backs like fingers crossed against a promise. Even though we know he's coming, we know better than to answer the door unprepared.

MEGHAN PHILLIPS is the author of the chapbook, *Abstinence Only* (Barrelhouse, 2019). Her stories and poems have been nominated for The Best of the Net, The Best Small Fictions anthology, and The Pushcart Prize. She lives in Lancaster, PA with her husband and son.

LIFECOLOR INDOOR LATEX PAINTS® - WHITES AND REDS

KRISTEN PLOETZ

Whites

Arrival

Hospital Light – AR101
Doctor's Coat – AR102
Swaddle – AR103
Midnight Feed – AR104
Nonna's Smile – AR105

First Year

Burp Cloth – FY201
First Tooth – FY202
Lost Lamby – FY203
Slice of Moon – FY204
Birthday Cake – FY205

Childhood

Sidewalk Chalk – CH301
Undertow (formerly Riptide) – CH302
Dandelion Fuzz – CH303
Broken Femur – CH304
Vanilla Cone – CH305

Adolescence

32AA – AD401
All-Star Laces – AD402
Mother's Best Sheets – AD403
Bleach – AD404
Levonorgestrel 0.75mg
    (formerly Morning After) – AD405

Young Adult I

Favorite T-Shirt – YA501
Beer Foam – YA502
Piña Colada – YA503
Benzoylmethylecgonine – YA504
Academic Dismissal – YA505

Young Adult II

Escitalopram 10 mg – YA506
Whitecaps – YA507
Full Dress Whites – YA508
Honorable Discharge – YA509
Size 10 Envelope – YA510

Middle Age

Latte (formerly Waitress Apron) – MA601
Rolling Papers – MA602
Lab Results – MA603
Silicone (Textured) – MA604
Jib Sail – MA605

Senior Years

Empty Pillow – SY701
Bichon Frise – SY702
Broken Hip – SY703
Windowpane – SY704
Soup of the Day – SY705

Departure

Sissy's Handkerchief – DE801
Hospital Blanket – DE802
Knuckles – DE803
Nurse's Sleeve – DE804
Clock Face – DE805

Reds

Learn

Gumball – LN101
Cardinal – LN102
Lost Balloon – LN103
Bicycle – LN104
Skinned Knee – LN105

Live + Leap

Drugstore Valentine – LI201
Menarche – LI202
Rum Punch – LI203
First Bite (formerly Hickey) – LI204
Popped Cherry – LI205

Love

Heart-Shaped Box – LV301
Matching Tattoos – LV302
Push-Up Bra – LV303
Poppy Bouquet – LV304
Dog-Eared Dostoevsky – LV305

Lose

Beer Pong Cup – LS401
2009 Chevy Impala – LS402
4-Way Stop – LS403
Tail Light – LS404
Myocardial Contusion – LS405

Lament

Bloodshot – LA501
Slit Wrist – LA502
Ruby Slippers – LA503
Venlafaxine Hydrochloride 150 mg – LA504
Nana's Patchwork Quilt – LA505

Lust + Lie

Stiletto – LU601
Pouty Lip (formerly Lipstick) – LU602
Satin Tie – LU603
Wife's Scream – LU604
Blocked Call – LU605

Leave + Land
- Cat Eye Frames – LE701
- Laser Removal – LE702
- Sublet Kitchen – LE703
- Subway Seat – LE704
- Potted Geraniums – LE705

KRISTEN M. PLOETZ is a former attorney and lives in Massachusetts. She is working on a collection of short stories, and is Creative Nonfiction Editor for *Atlas + Alice*. You can find links to her other publications at www.kristenploetz.com.

BREATHLESSNESS
CLAIRE POLDERS

I smother the moth in a jar, just to see it shrivel. But at night the moth revives, ghosting my dreams and infesting my imagination. One day, I awake to the sound of crinkling paper, and the moth, an infinite origami of stories, wraps its wings around my mouth.

CLAIRE POLDERS is the author of four novels in Dutch and co-author of one novel for younger readers (*A Whale in Paris*, Atheneum / Simon&Schuster, 2018). Her short work appeared in *Electric Literature*, *Tin House*, *TriQuarterly*, *Denver Quarterly*, and elsewhere. Find her online at www.clairepolders.com.

AND SOMETIMES WE MEET
DINA L. RELLES

You're alone on the road when the scraping sound starts to drown out Elliott Smith coming through the car radio. You're on your way to a work thing, your nerves already shot. You take the next exit—cursing yourself for being cheap, for only driving hand-me-downs—and find the gas station in a drowsy nowhere town.

When you examine the front passenger side, you see a large piece of black plastic hanging between the two front wheels. You don't know what it is or what it does. You know nothing about cars.

Someone in the next lane over takes notice, takes pity on you—eight months pregnant and crouching under your car—hollers he'll run in and find a gas station attendant.

He finds no one. Says he'll check it out himself.

His coat, the color of cornfields in winter, is creased along the hemline, the way it always gets after long stretches of sitting. He has a familiar face and corner-wrinkles at his eyes like the man who laid you down on his floor one old August night.

The stranger bends low, knees to earth, and you

worry about his pants.

"It's part of your underbody shield," he says. "Car'll run fine without it. But you have to cut it off or it could catch fire. Wait here." He runs between the gas pumps to his car and returns with a pocketknife.

He throws himself to the ground, starts slicing away at the sagging plastic. A couple other travelers have gathered by now. For a moment, you're all going nowhere together. Beyond them are houses set into hills with lights that flicker come dark, people who may never meet at a roadside gas station or anywhere else.

Back on his feet, he wipes away sweat even though it's autumn, hands you the severed piece—black and dirt-flecked and frayed around the edges.

"You don't need it," he says. "But take it with you, just in case."

This is your approach to all things, so you nod and say *Thank you* and you want to say more, maybe throw your arms around his neck or cry a little into his chest. But you climb back into the old car, quieted now, and curve onto the highway, thinking about him and everyone and the whole lonely-together world.

DINA L. RELLES' work has appeared in *Matchbook*, *Monkeybicycle*, *Hobart*, *Cheap Pop*, *River Teeth*, *DIAGRAM*, and *Wigleaf*, among others, and has been nominated for a Pushcart Prize. She is the Nonfiction Editor at *Pidgeonholes* and an Assistant Prose Poetry Editor at *Pithead Chapel*. More at www.dinarelles.com or @DinaLRelles.

DOMESTIC

BELINDA RIMMER

The problem with legs that won't go is they won't go. There was a time I could dance a night away with an exactness of step. I could kick a high-fandango, pirouette and split-jump across a room. But not anymore. Life can knock you about. It's a bossy school teacher forcing you to do math when you'd rather write a sonnet, which, by the way, has counting in it.

People, and by people I mean doctors, can't find a cure or a reason. Their quitting came slowly, after rounds of drug therapy and creams and hours in stuffy consulting rooms. I understand their frustration, I really do.

I've been seeing a psychiatrist called Gerald. We're on first name terms. He's almost completely rotund, like a barrel, the sort you see in a pub pretending to be a table.

Because I'm a difficult customer, I see him twice a week. The weeks have turned into years— three to be exact. He thinks the ocean of pain in my legs has nothing to do with my childhood—although there are Oedipal issues we address on a regular basis. This morning Gerald asked me, "If your legs could carry you away, where would they take you?"

I thought of Tenerife. But if you could choose one place in the world to visit, it shouldn't be Tenerife. I almost said Butlins. Gerald would have had a field day with Butlins, all those childhood memories. Instead, I shined the buttons on my coat.

By the time my husband came to fetch me, I was sobbing. He doesn't usually come to fetch me. Someone, maybe the receptionist, must have phoned him. He placed a damp hand on my shoulder, gave me a squeeze—a threat.

BELINDA is a widely published poet with a love of short fiction. She's made long and short lists in competitions and has a few stories published. She came second in the Ambit Poetry competition, 2018. Her pamphlet, *Touching Sharks in Monaco*, will be published by Indigo Dreams in 2019.

CRUMBS

NICOLE RIVAS

A week before Anna planned to die, we stood in my kitchen making eggplant parmigiana. She'd already divulged her morbid desire to me days prior, certain I would keep her secret. For some reason, I did; we were two eggs whisked. I thought our dinner date would change her mind—the smell of eggplant crisping in olive oil, Pavarotti exploding on the record player, limoncello in old jam jars. What about this life wasn't to love? I laid a red-and-white-checkered cloth on the table. Anna smirked as I complained about the lumps of egg and breadcrumb between my fingers. I watched her pale hands as she patted excess grease off the gold medallions of eggplant, Anna herself a treasure. I pulled one of her greasy hands to my face and kissed it on the knuckles. Those knuckles were cold. Anna made the joke about the warm heart and smiled, pulled her hand away.

At Anna's funeral, everyone brought food. Nieces with bruschetta, aunts with penne arrabbiata, an estranged uncle with *frutti di mare*. The clams stank in the hot sun. Anna's family mourned at her casket and ate after the burial, right there in the grass next to the six-foot-deep hole and the two-foot-tall photo of Anna when she was still a child, when she was still a Catholic. Grandmas sat next to the hole on lawn chairs, crying with spaghetti sauce on their chins. Young cousins fought over pizza, too confused about death to really think about it. Parents toothed the edges of their blue Solo cups. Even the priest had a plate. Though not family, not even Italian or Italian American, I ate right along with all of Anna's relatives. No one asked who I was, and I was too upset to speak, certain we were all here because of what I had done, which was nothing.

Roma tomatoes, fresh linguine, garlic marinara, spicy meatballs. The smell of freshly turned earth was a seasoning no one wanted, but it had infiltrated everything, even the cheesy armor of the ziti. And once it was in, it was in.

NICOLE RIVAS teaches writing in Savannah, GA and holds an MFA in Creative Writing from The University of Alabama. Her chapbook of flash fiction, *A Bright and Pleading Dagger*, was the winner of the Rose Metal Press 12th Annual Short Short Chapbook Contest. For more, visit www.nicolemrivas.com.

from PANK

BABY DOLLS

BECKY ROBISON

My mother isn't always Raggedy Ann, but she was when I was born. Week before Halloween, office party. Not at the office, but at Richard Nixon's basement apartment. She sipped on Shirley Temples while my jelly fists pommeled her beneath her denim thrift-store jumper. I hate grenadine, but how was Raggedy Ann supposed to know that? Her brain was stuffing, and my communication was limited to pathetic fetal boxing. The drunk guests rollicked in their altered states. When fluid dampened her striped stockings, everyone laughed. Because she was a doll, and also very young, my mother laughed, too.

A cat whose tail was longer than her skirt laid Raggedy Ann in the bathtub and closed the moldy curtain. Her limbs stayed limp while people pissed nearby, and the tangled nest of red yarn remained on her head, drenched with sweat, for Raggedy Ann is loyal and true. Only I was able to bring her to life, each shock of me making bone and blood of her soft body, carving chambers into her two-dimensional valentine heart.

BECKY ROBISON is a Chicago native and a graduate of UNLV's Creative Writing MFA program. Her fiction has appeared in journals like *Paper Darts* and *Midwestern Gothic*, and she also serves as Social Media and Marketing Coordinator for *Split Lip Magazine*. She's currently working on a novel.

DESERT MOTEL

BRAD ROSE

Today is fever bright, no wind. Justine says I should slow down, but I speed up. I like to get to things before they get to me. She's been searching for her birthmother. It's taken her about two years to get this far. I tell her she probably won't recognize her. She laughs and says, *Curtis, not every day has to be a maybe.* Everybody wants something real. When we get to Vegas, she opens her purse and pulls out a birth certificate. It's a single page, and on the back, it has tiny ink footprints and a large thumbprint. The motel is pink and white, and our room is cold as a skating rink. I sit on the end of one of the twin beds, drinking a Cherry Coke. Outside, it's 102 in the shade. The pool is filled with screaming kids. You can hear them having fun, or something like it. I remind Justine there are more plastic flamingos in the world than real ones.

BRAD ROSE is the author of a collection of poetry and flash fiction, *Pink X-Ray* (Big Table Publishing, 2015, pinkx-ray. com and Amazon.com.) His new two new books of poetry, *Momentary Turbulence* and *WordinEdgeWise*, are forthcoming from Cervena Barva Press. Brad's website is: www. bradrosepoetry.com from CINCINNATI REVIEW

NOT SORRY
SARAH SALWAY

He is so much smaller than her that she gets embarrassed, wondering if from behind he looks like her child, a hunched-up boy in adult clothes like some kind of war refugee, and if so, when he kisses her, will strangers gasp, hurry past so they can see her from the front, and he does kiss her often because it makes him smile to stand on tiptoe, to reach up and take her by the shoulders that are so much wider than his own, and though in anyone else, her reluctance to meet his lips would be cruel, it seems to make him more determined, although she's never told him about the child thing, or how once, when she saw their shared reflection in the glass, he looked like a little wizened monkey climbing up her great stout oak of a tree, and how she would have pushed him off straight away but he stopped kissing her suddenly, bent down to wipe the dust off the tips of his black leather shoes, such small shoes, and she stood still, looking at the reflection, just her now, alone, the moon making a perfect halo around her head, and her lips were tingling so much that in the window she saw her hand come up and touch them, her tingling lips, her fingertips smoothing her mouth like applying a salve, searching in vain for the one spot, any spot, he'd missed.

SARAH SALWAY has written three novels (including *Something Beginning With*) and is a short story writer and poet. A former Canterbury Laureate, her work has been translated into several languages and her poetry has appeared in financial newspapers, public parks and postcards, as well as in book form. www.sarahsalway.co.uk

WORLD'S FINEST

KIM SAMSIN

When you were tiny, I watched you sleep and made promises. You will do the same; you will vow there is no wall you would not tear down, no jungle you would not clear. Your imagination will fail you. Someday, I will remind you of this: you brought home boxes of World's Finest Chocolate bars from school, pack after cloying pack, and I told you I would take them to work to sell for you. Every day you brought home more. I tried to sell them, I did, but every parent in town had their own chocolate burden. I canceled my hair appointment. 20 dollars. I sold your father's comic books. 60 dollars. I told his mother she would never see you again if she didn't buy a box. *24 dollars' worth of chocolate, Carolyn, really?* "Worth" is the wrong word for it, but yes. 24 dollars. That was the month we lived on spaghetti and I let you sleep in your blanket fort so that I could turn down the thermostat. I hid the boxes in my closet, in an old hardside suitcase, and hoped they wouldn't attract mice. I stacked them in my filing cabinet at work. I stored six boxes in my car trunk and then the temperature spiked and I had the world's finest plaque of chocolate and carpet fibers and almonds and foil wrappers. The waxy, sweet smell imbued everything I touched. And you won. I won. I came home from work and you were sitting on the floor in front of Woody Woodpecker, your legs splayed out, your glasses smeared and slipping off your nose, and you launched yourself at me. It was the last time you hugged me like that, your face in my belly, your arms around my waist. Three days later, I stood at the side of the hockey rink while a man lifted you up and put you on the back of a Zamboni. Most of the audience was filing out for intermission. Someone announced your name over the loudspeaker. *77 boxes of candy sold*, they said, *a school record, congratulations going out to Kevin*. The arena speakers boomed with "Eye of the Tiger" and they drove that machine over the ice at about three miles an hour and you shook your raised fists in the air.

KIM SAMSIN is an editor in Winnipeg, Manitoba.

from SYNAESTHESIA MAGAZINE

THE END OF THE WORLD
NOA SIVAN

They meet on a hookup app. He sends her the same question he asks everyone else: "The world's ending tomorrow and only you know. Do you share this knowledge or keep it to yourself to prevent chaos?"

And she answers: "So you know, too."

NOA SIVAN was born and raised in Israel and is currently living in Granada, Spain. She's a graphic designer, writer and assistant editor for *Cheap Pop literary journal*. She tweets under the handle @migdalorr.

WHAT I NOW KNOW

RACHEL SMITH

If the new year brings a heavy fruiting of vī, the risk of a cyclone increases and your boat from the north will not be able to dock at Avatiu Wharf.

A wasp can sting at any time, even my arm that snakes around your waist as we ride, clockwise, on and on. A flower snapped from a tīpani tree oozes white sap which will not ease the swelling.

At 3am the moon lays down its silver.

The tuna I buy in thick red slabs may or may not have eaten a smaller fish whose stomach was clogged with toothbrush bristles.

A coconut that falls in the night can crack a pig's head right open but kuru will spill its own grey matter across the damp earth. Chickens will peck at either.

What I have yet to learn is everything.

When I hitch my pareu high and wash my fanny at the tap around the back of the house, your neighbour and I can pretend we never saw each other.

A boat can slip its moorings and leave without sound so that out past the lagoon, past the white rim of the reef, there is nothing but ocean.

Rain falls heavy when no one is watching. My sheets will smell of your damp skin for weeks.

GLOSSECTOMY

RACHEL SMITH

The phone rang on and on until finally, on what had become day five, its battery ran out. Outside, birdsong and buffeting winds, but in here it was as if you'd taken my tongue when you closed the door; that your bags held more than just your share that we'd divvied up so politely—power tools and photo albums and worn tea towels laid out on the living room floor. It had made me want to play Twister again—left foot on the Ben Harper CD you hummed when you were happy, right foot on the tent we set up in a toilet block the night Lake Matheson flooded, left hand on the remains of your Mum's dinner set after I threw the lot at your head that night you never came home at all, and your right hand, the one that touched me, set down in a slick pool of unable to face the facts, you need to get your shit sorted, that you had left me to soak in. Day 10 broken syllables backed up against the stub of my tongue. I ran out of cat food and sent her off towards the shed whose mouse population we had never managed to curb. You took our speakers and the flat screen, but I found the scarf I'd knitted for your birthday three years ago stuffed into the letterbox. Like everything else I'd had visions—sheep grazing on soft green pastures, your arms held a metre apart as I wove skeins around them, our hands slippery with the scent of husbandry.

RACHEL SMITH'S work has been published in journals and anthologies in Aotearoa New Zealand and overseas. She has been short listed for the Bath Flash Fiction Award and TSS International Flash Fiction, and placed second in 2017 NZ National Flash Fiction Day.

THE SEEDS OF THINGS
JOE P. SQUANCE

When the condom got stuck in the vending machine in the basement of his dorm and he grabbed one side and she grabbed the other—both of them just a little bit drunk, trying pointlessly to be quiet while getting ready to make a whole lot of noise, his body electrified with the prospect of imminent sex and who knows what occurring chemically within her—it occurred to him suddenly that none of this was happening, that neither of them was really there and that he was only an echo, my memory of myself, knocked loose by anxiety, by the roiling and churning blood in my brain as I pinched the skin of her belly between my fingers and slid in a syringe. She cried then, there in our bedroom, in the moment and not in the memory. It was painful. She'd done the smaller injections herself—poking them into the thick skin of her thigh, thumbing down the depressors, pulling the needles out and handing them to me. I was there for support. I swabbed the injection sites and collected the waste. But this shot was not like the others: the site was more sensitive, the syringe—full of hormones to trigger ovulation, which I imagined as a bloom unfurling—more severe.

This one hurt. It would be worth it, I told her. It would be worth it, I told us both. If it doesn't work, she said, I'm not sure I can go through all this again, and my brain flooded once more with hot blood. I returned to the memory of those two kids, their bodies flush, standing astride a basement vending machine, and I watched them rock that thing back and forth and back and forth until they got exactly what it was that they wanted.

JOE P. SQUANCE is a very slow writer of very short stories, and an adjunct instructor of creative writing. His stories have appeared in *Atticus Review*, *Cease, Cows*, *Everyday Fiction*, *Fiction Southeast*, and elsewhere. He lives in Oxford, Ohio with his wife and their young daughter.

TSUNAMI
ELIZABETH STIX

She had a setback. She suffered a blow. She had a string of personal misfortunes. There was the toner cartridge, shaken when the plastic tab was already off, her cream silk blouse, her boss' contact lens. That was a mishap. There was the oil running low, so she checked it, and she added it, but she left the engine cap off, and the smoke wafted up but there was no stopping on the bridge, and she didn't know why they said that but she figured it was so you would not get hit. She read about a guy who pulled over on the bridge when he got rear-ended and the accident didn't kill him but another car hit his car and his car rolled forward and hit him and that threw him over the railing and he fell into the ocean. So she knew better than to stop. There was the callus remover blade she bought off of QVC that was a Smart Razor, that said it shaved away only callused skin; it was so smart it knew to stop at soft skin; it wouldn't cut it. That was an unfortunate accident. There was the blind date that was going so well, a new leaf, a light at the end of the tunnel, so well that she excused herself from her clam linguini and went into the restroom to put in her diaphragm right then and there, no awkward pauses later. She popped the case and lubed the rubber cup's soft rim. She put one foot on the toilet and pinched the bendy sides together; saw it sproing out of her hand and hit the wall, roll across the tiles and slip beneath the gap under the door into the restaurant, onto the green and yellow carpet. That was a misadventure. That was a regret.

ELIZABETH STIX'S stories have appeared in *McSweeney's, Tin House, Eleven Eleven, The Fabulist,* and the *Los Angeles Times* Sunday Magazine. Her story "Alice" won the Bay Guardian Fiction Prize and was optioned by Sneaky Little Sister Films. She is finishing a novel-in-stories called *Things I Want Back from You.*

MASCULINITIES
PAUL STROHM

Sailor Doll

My father was edgy about my Christmas request for a doll. "Gol-darnit," he was saying to my mother, "where does that kid get his ideas?" What was the problem? My sister had a dozen and I was only asking for one. Innocent of the role of sailors in the gay imagination, he decided the answer was to get me a sailor doll. I named him "Petey." The first thing I did was shrink his wool uniform in my sister's doll washing machine. I took him to school anyway, for show and tell, unclad except for pinched-looking little black sailor oxfords.

Footballer

Ever hopeful, my father bought me a kid-sized football uniform, complete with ungainly plastic shoulder pads and an ear-crunching, vision-obscuring helmet. He dressed me up in it and sent me down to the vacant lot where the neighborhood kids ran a pickup game. Briefly awed by my official-looking getup, they abandoned previous custom and handed me the ball. For a long five or six seconds all of us stood there, frozen, wondering whether my costume had transformed me into a credible athlete. Then they recollected themselves, unceremoniously threw me to the ground, and punched away any thought of equipment-based advantage.

Some Car

I meant to buy a practical sedan. I came home with a mean-looking Chevy Camaro instead. Not much of a back seat, but the children were still small. I settled for the six-cylinder model. "Some car," my friends said. "Like Paul," my wife said. "Looks good but not much under the hood." No wonder that marriage didn't last. My next car was a Prelude, also low slung. Claire was sitting in it at the gas station. She became convinced that a guy was hanging around and ogling her. I gave him a look. He said, "You wanna sell that car?"

PAUL STROHM divides his time between Brooklyn and Oxford. He has taught literature and humanities at Columbia, Oxford, and Indiana. He has recently published a biography of Chaucer (Viking-Penguin) and a book on Conscience (Oxford University Press). His story collection is available on Amazon, as *Sportin' Jack: 100 100-Word Stories*.

PRINCESSES

XENIA TAIGA

In their beds the princesses complained about pins and needles. The men collected all the cardboard, plywood, tissue rolls, and bubble wrap; installing it and packing it around them tightly. The princesses slept better, but it was not perfect. At night their feet turned into ice, while their bodies burned. The men brought their axes and chopped off their feet. They curled up in bed keeping the feet secured between their chins and chests. In the mornings the feet would be lost in the sheets or fallen to the floor. It was still not perfect. The men gazed at the ceiling as the princesses spoke, wishing the men would listen to them. They used their knives to slice off their ears and wrapped them up in soft tissue paper. In the mornings when the princesses woke up, they presented their gifts. The princesses opened their offerings, the papers soiled and heavy with their blood, flitted their eyelashes and said, *Thank you.* Later, they learned the language of hands. In silence the women weaved tales airing out their grievances. They realized high up in their tower, unable to walk or clip away the ivy strands crowding the window view, they couldn't see the birds. They've been very unlucky and asked for luck. The men went into the woods to find a rabbit. Finding one, they slaughtered it. Leaving behind its body in the forest, they marched home to bring the good fortune. The princesses slept holding the rabbit foot in one hand and their feet in the other, but in the morning they woke up complaining of their dreams and nightmares; of how hands poked and probed them, of how shadows transformed into bodies demanding to be in their presence. The men thought long and hard and finally decided that the hands must be cut off as well. The men stretched the princesses' legs and arms tying them tight to their bedposts. Then they tenderly laid the rabbit foot, their cold feet, and their hands around their heads on the pillows like a halo. The women, tired and worn out, decided it was not worth being princesses anymore and closed their eyes; not even bothering to hear the birds chirping just outside their windows.

XENIA TAIGA lives in southern China with a cockatiel, a turtle and an Englishman. She's currently at work on a novel. xeniataiga.com

THE HAIR CHILD

KAJ TANAKA

When you shave your cat, you make a new cat, a better cat. And when you shave your son, you make a new son who emerges screaming into this world—a hair child made from your son's hair a more compliant, more loving, less complaining version of your son.

During that first night, the hair child stirs in his sleep. He knows his origin story and it troubles him even during the first night, even more as he grows bigger and stronger. He is afraid of his brother, the human; he is afraid of himself; he is afraid of you. Yet you are lost in the awe you feel for him. He tells you his dreams but they make no sense—low whistles, he says, the curves of cold statues in the darkness, but then, the hair child can only speak in short sentences and he knows very few words so it is possible that he feels more than he can relate. It is also possible that he feels nothing.

You do not give the hair child a name because to name him might encourage him somehow. You do not know what he is capable of, your hair golem.

Your son tells the children at school about his brother who has no name and speaks haltingly like a baby. No one believes him, he says. He is crying at the dinner table saying no one believes him. Please let me take him to school, he begs you. You ask the hair child if it wants to go to school with its brother. *No*, it says. But the hair child, like all children, is resistant to change. You think school would do the hair child good, but it is stubborn and it will not go. You say that the matter is settled. The hair child will go to school. The hair child slithers away.

The next morning you find that the hair child has braided itself into a long coil and has wrapped itself around a leg of the dining room table like a python. *I won't be going anywhere today*, screams the hair child. You look over and see what it has done. Fine, you say, but if you don't go, there will be no more dinner and there will be no more talking. *Fine*, says the hair child, *I never liked dinner and I never liked talking.*

When your son returns from school and finds the hair child silently wrapped around the leg of the dining room table, he begs it to come to school with him the next day. He attempts to appeal to its sense of fraternal obligation. He says that the other children have been making fun of him ever since he mentioned his brother who is made of hair. You can see your son is upset, but you are not talking, and the hair child is not talking. Your son screams, and his scream is like the sound of another hair child being born.

And alone, alone, finally alone the next day, you shave your head, and each of your hairs screams into being; your curling locks squirm across the bathroom floor like worms, each with a mind, each with a body. And you can make more. In a few months or a year, if you need to, you can make more.

KAJ TANAKA is a PhD candidate at the University of Houston. His stories have been selected for Best Small Fictions and nominated for the Pushcart Prize. He is the fiction editor at *Gulf Coast*. You can read more of his work at kajtanaka. com and tweet to him @kajtanaka

MY FATHER COMFORTS ME IN THE FORM OF BIRDS

SHARON TELFER

Heron

The December tarmac's glazing treacherous black. My mind should be on the road, not with my mother, left in the echoing house.

I take the roundabout too fast.

There it is, standing guard. I've never seen one here. No water, only frozen fields. Sentinel grey, crunched into its awkward bones, those quilling eyebrows. Unmistakable.

I hear his voice.

"*Hamba gashle.*"

"*What's that, Dad?*"

"*It's Zulu. It means…*"

I whisper it back as the light fades.

"*…Go safely.*"

I flip the visor against the falling sun.

Pheasant

We startle them into clattering flight. Survivors,

seeing the New Year in against the odds.

One stays grounded, escorts us like a maverick sheepdog hitching a walk.

That look. *"Dad?"* Joking.

It stops. Its feathers glint rainbows in the iced light.

That sideways look. *"Is that you, Dad?"* Half-joking.

The absurd lens of grief.

Sparrowhawk?

Hard to tell. We pass so quickly.

Roadside perch. Sharp eyes scanning.

"What do I always say?"

"Keep your options open, Dad."

Robin

On a clear day you can see the hills he loved from here.

This is not a clear day.

Every voice feels winter-stopped.

In the branches, a spot of red, defiant.

"The robin keeps singing right through the winter."

Its sweet strain clarifies the clouded air.

"Very few birds do that, you know."

The mist begins to lift, a little.

Goldfinch

The feeders have swung empty for months. We knock the nails in lower so Mum can reach, refill them with rich sunflower hearts.

"They're back!"

From the kitchen window we watch a charm of gold glitter the garden.

Curlew

Spring loops in on that cool, clear call, back to breed on the hard, high moors.

"That day we found a nest, remember? The baby curlew? The parent bird circling overhead?"

The wind lifts heady scent from the greening woods, scatters blossom like confetti, accepts the ash we offer.

Skylark

You hear it first, notes like diamonds etching glass.

Lift your head. Turn your face to the full sun.

"Look long enough, you will see it."

There, infinitesimal in the infinite blue.

Do you see him?

Yes! There! Rising, singing, rising...

SHARON TELFER has won the Bath Flash Fiction Award and, with 'My father comforts me in the form of birds', the Reflex Fiction Prize. In 2018, she was awarded the New Writing North/Word Factory Short Story Apprenticeship for emerging short story writers. She lives near York, UK.

THE CENTRAL LINE HAS SEVERE DELAYS

JAMIE THUNDER

The radio alarm, the hurried breakfast, the quick kiss goodbye, the waiting train, the familiar cabin, the tired passengers, Ealing Broadway, Lancaster Gate, Oxford Circus, the platform, the young man, the step the sudden thud the brakes the brakes the brakes the screams the sick the distant voice the arm to hold on to, the hot sweet tea, the soft words, the phonecalls, the clock, the waiting, the arms, the words, the drive, the sleep, the waking, the sleep, the leaflets, the room, the man, the clasped hands, the exercises, the bad days, the good days, the bad days, the walls, the phonecalls, the excuses, the phonecalls, the excuses, the silence, the shouting, the heat, the slam, the taste, the first, the second, the third, the lies, the promise, the mints, the secrets, the table, the cans, the questions, the tears, the fist, the bag, the slam, the quiet, the relief, the silence, the hiss, the click, the hiss, the click, the days, the weeks, the walls, the meetings, the first day back, the handshakes, the headache, the flask, the cameras, the meeting, the letter, the reception desk, the corner office, the pleading, the punch, the crack, the hand, the march, the warning, the walk, the hiss, the click, the hiss, the click, the crowds, the roar of cars, the bridge, the jump, the rush of air—

JAMIE THUNDER lives, reads, and writes somewhere near London, and tries to behave better than his characters. He's been published by places like *Prole, Storgy,* and *Spelk Fiction,* and is one of The Short Story's selected writers for 2017/18. He also writes at asintheweather.wordpress.com and tweets as @jdthndr.

THE DELICATE ART
OF IKEBANA

CATHY ULRICH

If I were a florist in Japan, I would like flowering plum best, the paleness of it.

It represents hope, you know, I would say to my customers, who would nod politely, as if they didn't already know.

I would be so proficient at *ikebana*, placing flowers in vases just so. The *shin*, the *soe*, the *hikae*, the balance of emptiness and asymmetry.

You always smell like flowers, my Japanese boyfriend would say. I would never know if that meant he liked it or not.

If I were a florist in Japan, I would bring the leftover bouquets home to our 12-tatami apartment. There would be flowers on the counters, flowers on the floor. We would have to walk so very carefully. Flowers are so very delicate, after all.

From time to time, we would bump a vase, jostle the flowers within, ruin the line of the *shin*. From time to time, we would knock a vase to the ground, the shattering of glass like the quiet after an argument.

I would pick up the broken pieces with my bare hand, end up cutting myself so that my Japanese boyfriend would have to bandage my fingers, or do like they always do in manga, lick the wound.

Why do you always do this, he'd say. *Why don't you use a towel?*

If I were a florist in Japan, I wouldn't tell my Japanese boyfriend how much I liked these times when he fussed over me, my hands in his hands, his tongue on my fingertips.

I would only say: *I don't know.*

I would only say: *I'm sorry, I don't know, I'm sorry.*

If I were a florist in Japan, my Japanese boyfriend would drop my hands, reach for a towel, say: *It's all right.*

He'd say: *Don't worry, it's all right.*

He would help me get the broken glass into the recyclables. He would help me pick up the wounded flowers, one by one. We would step over the place where they had fallen, the emptiness there, the asymmetry.

You smell like flowers, my Japanese boyfriend would say. *You always smell like flowers.*

CATHY ULRICH is a writer from Montana. Her work has been published in various journals, including *Wigleaf, Passages North* and *Black Warrior Review*.

THERE WILL BE NO LACE

TM UPCHURCH

Your lips bubble and slurp, a sweet shik-shik suckle of air as I curl around you, smelling your butterscotch breath. You pause to gape a greedy smile, swallowing the night; you are ready for this life.

They tug at my shoulder. They say, Don't you be making a fuss, now.

I shrug them loose, lean in and swaddle you tight so you won't feel the cold. Pretend I'm still here. Your eyelids close, open, close, open less... As they slide down, sealing you into sleep, I am still here. I brand my mind with the moment, breathing in deep, sucking you into me before they take my wrists.

I flinch. No, no, they say, you know... (What you did. What happens now.)

I reach forward to whisper into your mouth, for you to taste my words; you were, are, will be loved... if I could—if I could reach, I would whisper.

They grip my elbows and my father nods.

Wheels on cobbles; my breath jolts and stops, and I have to make promises to coax the air back in. You'll grow up beautiful, I'll come back. While

I'm gone, I'll make lace napkins and pray to share a meal one day.

They teach me mea culpa, dress me in black and steer me down stone corridors. It's too late to marry your father so now I'm to marry God; I'll sleep under sorry-thin sheets and wake with cold sides. Each morning, I'll grow stone knees and give thanks for the walls around me. There will be no more children. There will be no visits home, not even the sad return of a widowed bride—not unless God dies before me.

They say, Pray for your sins.

I pray, rejoicing in the sin that made you. I pray you grow strong, pray that no one ever steers you by your arms, and I pray that you have your own napkins because they've told me already, there will be no lace.

TM UPCHURCH writes in a little house overlooking the Atlantic. Her short fiction has been published in print and online, and shortlisted for the Bridport Prize, Bath Flash Fiction Award, and HISSAC short story competition. She is working on her first novel. She tweets as @tmupchurch and blogs at www.tmupchurch.com.

MAKING AN ILLEGAL U-TURN ON 15TH NEAR UNION

ZACH VANDEZANDE

At a certain point you just have to go for it, and then you are hitting the kid, and you want to say the sound is like a plonk, but it's not. It's a sound outside of language, after all, and you feel that feeling that you are part of the car, that the car is your body colliding with the kid's body, and your own meaty body is just an organ in the vehicle, your awareness of it proprioceptive—like a fender is your limb and it is knocking the kid under and away. Not away enough. The tire clumping over a leg at the kneecap. The soundlessness of splintering bone. Think that a tire might be a cushion of air that bears all the force, that you might be part of something misguided but miraculous, before you hear the wail. Do not hear the wail. The wail requires, and you do not have anything to give it. Ask yourself what life meant until now and what it will mean after now. Wonder at what point your belief in yourself as a person becomes insufficient, and if this is that point. A bike will clatter under you, and here comes the second rise and fall, the back tire adding injury to injury, here comes the onlook and the limblessness and the official response and then the shame-shouldered slump of the rest of your life.

ZACH VANDEZANDE is an author and professor. He lives in Ellensburg, Washington (sometimes) and Washington, DC (sometimes). He is the author of a novel, *Apathy and Paying Rent* (Loose Teeth Press, 2008), and a forthcoming short story collection, *Liminal Domestic: Stories* (Gold Wake Press, 2019). He knows all the dogs in his neighborhood.

SATIN NIGHTWEAR FOR WOMEN IRREGULAR

ELISABETH INGRAM WALLACE

The walk to the Allotment is wet and full of cats, taut muscled screams darting under cars. It's clunky, carrying all the bulbs she hoarded in one plastic bag, a bin-liner, stretched to a thin translucent skin.

When I get to her plot, I plant them. 10 halogen, 22 bayonet, and 37 screw bulbs.

The ground around me is worming, and when I walk away the earth shatters.

I take her two nightstand drawers full of polyester nightwear to the wasteland behind Lidl. Giant white French knickers, black slips, a blood red chemise.

The labels are cheap and Chinese and the brands don't translate. "Queen Silky Unique," "Satin Nightwear for Women Irregular."

I squirt lighter fluid, drop a lit match. When I walk away the sky bites and coughs through me. I can taste the perfume burn, her tight satin cling.

Her cookbooks next; 123.

One is handwritten.

Her life in cakes, pages clotted with butter, her

fingerprints, still. Two sheets stick, crack open an echo; a Rorschach of coffee, spilt decades ago—cockroach, demon, shadows. Her face.

Next day, I walk past it, already displayed in the Oxfam window. 99 pence.

For three weeks, I walk home a different way.

I walk the long, wrong way home and think of another window, the one in the hospital. I opened it wide. "My wife is too hot," I'd said to the nurse, "she needs air."

But I needed air. I didn't want to be alone in that room, with her last breath. I wanted it out.

I tell everyone. I am OK.

Burying her is easy.

It's just filling a hole. Burning her up into sky, and walking away.

ELISABETH INGRAM WALLACE has writing in *SmokeLong Quarterly*, *Atticus Review*, *Flash Frontier*, and elsewhere. A Senior Editor for the *Best British and Irish Flash Fiction*, her stories have won the Scottish Book Trust 'New Writers Award', a 'Dewar Arts Award', 'Writing the Future', and the TSS Flash Fiction Competition.

HELPING
CLARE WEZE

Leave the car bravely when you come across the injured barn owl. Your first sighting. Owning the middle of the road, owning the night too, but caught out, injured and flapping while your carload, warm from the pub, stares uselessly, even the driver.

Announce to your pals that you'll coax it into the side. Take determined, careful strides, all the while imagining how you'll carry the grateful creature to safety. Because you surely can. The thrashing and flailing increase, getting nowhere, but still, you can save the day. Night.

The damaged wing is obvious now. That wing will not refold. Hold out your hand. Stare into those dark eyes, marvel at that impossibly white face, whitened further in the headlights. Don't even wonder about the *how* of it—was it knocked by another car? Attacked? Did it simply misjudge a barrier? Just act.

When it lunges, eyes never leaving yours, stagger back a step. When, despite the pain in that limply hanging wing, it jabs at you again, then reels from you a second later, dipping its head—make soothing noises. Stand your ground. When a barn owl dips its head like that, is it showing submission? Why don't you know?

Say, "I'm sorry."

Say, "I just want to help."

When it dips again as if in answer, apologise once more and know that every soul has frozen: the mesmerised carload; the barn owl; and you in the road, big, frightening and useless.

CLARE WEZE'S forthcoming short story collection won a Northern Writers' Award, and she is a Bridport shortlistee (flash). Her short fiction has been published by *Aesthetica*, *Ad Hoc Fiction*, *Commonword*, *The Conglomerate*, *Wonderbox*, *Bridge House*, *Bare Fiction* and *Reflex Fiction*. She is represented by The Good Literary Agency. clareweze.com @ ClareWeze

THE LAUNDRY ROOM COMES FIRST

CHARMAINE WILKERSON

If you believe that the key events in a man's life should be recounted in their order of occurrence, then the laundry room comes first, followed by your sudden move to a new country, followed by a wife, a divorce, your involvement in local politics, your remarriage, the scandal surrounding that clandestine dump for toxic waste, a courtroom trial, your bankruptcy, your comeback with a reality TV show and, finally, a murder-suicide in your beachside home.

If, instead, you believe that the story of a life should begin with the happening of greatest significance, then my tale, too, starts in the laundry room, with my death at age four, 30 years before you take your own life, thus easing some of my grief over the untimely loss of myself, and resolving that early crisis point in the plot where my mouth, finally mature enough to articulate such things, reports the murder of my childhood, only to find its cries of foul play falling on deaf ears.

If, as some hope, a life can be resurrected through selective memory, then my only story will, necessarily, begin where I run out of the laundry room to chase lizards in the dirt, to hopscotch in the driveway, to side-step a fat toad on a wet lawn, to read books to a toy giraffe, to ride a bicycle with foot brakes and, back on the cool floor of the laundry room, to witness the birth of six tender-voiced puppies, sliding into the amber light of a warm morning, eyes still swollen shut yet knowing how to find the teat, where to seek their sustenance, where to begin their story.

CHARMAINE WILKERSON'S novella *How to Make a Window Snake* has won the Bath Novella-in-Flash Award and the Saboteur Award for Best Novella. Her microfiction can be found in various literary magazines and anthologies. Originally from New York, she has lived in several cities and is currently based in Italy.

from ATTICUS REVIEW

HALF TANK

BENJAMIN WOODARD

The old lady shook. A gas hose, detached from the pump, chased her rear bumper like a rat's tail. People drive off with the nozzles all the time, the attendant said, it's no big deal. Still, the police came. Listened. Covered the spill with kitty litter. The lady swore she meant no harm, said the incident was a case of forgetfulness, a senior moment, but the police hauled her away after she got feisty and spat on their shoes. Francisco saw the whole thing from across the street. He couldn't stop laughing, and tonight, he sits in his open window at home and draws cartoons of the scene, only in his version the pump is on fire. Explosive. Francisco's older brother Elijah dances with citronella candles on the deck below. They are free because their parents have now been gone a week, and Francisco wonders if, like the old lady, they too forgot about the tethers in their lives before they fled. He looks up. A moth with a punctured wing beats within his reach. Dogs bark. Meanwhile, Elijah's shadow spreads across the vinyl siding like gasoline on hot asphalt.

BENJAMIN WOODARD is editor-in-chief at *Atlas and Alice* Literary Magazine. He lives in Connecticut with his wife and teaches English. His stories have appeared in *Hobart*, *Monkeybicycle*, *Atticus Review*, and other journals. Find him online at benjaminjwoodard.com.

REVERSE FIELD TRIP

LUKE WORTLEY

There is the needle. Before that, there is an equine veterinarian preparing a lethal dose of sodium pentobarbital.

Before that, there is a magnificent Bay thoroughbred named Frankly My Dear in a trailer, pupils stretched and oblivious, hips and ribcage palpitating to metallic crackles as the truck ahead trots forward.

Before that, there is a child named Maximiliano in critical condition at Kosair Children's Hospital. Before that, there is an ambulance ride down the Watterson Expressway with an EMT and a hellish concoction of heaves, maledictions, prayers.

Before that, there is a call to Maximiliano's padres, Socorro y Juan Manuel. Before that, there is a group of other children silent as sleeping dogs, watching their friend leak onto the fresh asphalt.

Before that, there is a connection of low-moisture keratin capped with aluminum with its close cousin, the high-moisture keratinocyte compound stretched over just a few cubic centimeters of collagen and calcium phosphate, otherwise known as the cheek bone of a four-year-old at Jeffersontown Christian

Church preschool.

Before that, there is a tug on the twitching tail. Before that, there is a completely calm horse and an exuberant child in the parking lot of a Disciples of Christ Church next to Veteran's Park. Before that, there is snack time and a giddy line of jacketed children cantering into the parking lot.

Before that, Layla and Maximiliano hand in permission slips.

Before that, there is a paper sent home detailing an end-of-year, reverse field trip where the animals come to them.

Before that, there is one set of parents, Layla's mom and dad, just trying to be nice, checking the box, folding an extra few dollars for their daughter to bring to Ms. Jennifer. Before that, there is another set of parents, Socorro and Juan Manuel de Soto Vega, preparing to attend la misa at St. Catherine's, assuring Max that, por seguro, no hay problema. Ya vamos.

Before that, there are two last-minute addenda to the form, one adding the option for parent/guardian to sponsor another child's reverse field trip and another for parent/guardian to give permission but request sponsorship, anonymously.

When LUKE was in high school, he wanted to be an interventional radiologist. After a few concussions, he forgot calculus and began playing with words. He has an MFA in Creative Writing from Butler University, where he teaches Latin American history. Follow him on Twitter @LukeWortley and lukewortley.com.

FEEDING TIME

TARA ISABEL ZAMBRANO

Almost spring, and a sparrow hits the fan and falls into the mutton curry while we're having lunch. Papa says it's something to do with feeding her chicks, the bird's always in a hurry. I pick up and carry the stunned little creature to the bed where Papa and Ma don't sleep together anymore.

Year after year these sparrows have been making nests in that corner of the living room—one morning a broken egg on the floor, yolk clinging to the fractured shell. The same week Ma woke up in a pool of blood and cried for weeks because it was a boy.

Every few days, Ma cleans the bird shit stuck on the floor and the wall. Back in the nest, the mother's at attention, a rush of wings as if responding to Ma's curses. Some days the sparrow sits on the fence, flies around, swoops this way and that, shows off.

Now the bird lies on her side, breathing hard, until she puffs her gravy-stained chest and stands up. Before I help Ma to dispose the mutton curry—the only food we had because we're down to single meals a day since Papa got fired last month, I check on her again—and sure enough she's back in the nest, peeping at our empty dining table.

NEW OLD
TARA ISABEL ZAMBRANO

Before your mother's death, your father sat anywhere in the living room. Afterward, he'd place himself where he could see the urn holding her ashes. One day, he scoops out a tablespoon of ash and mixes it with his tea. Then he sits outside, up to his face in the pink evening as the light falls away.

A week later, when your father starts wearing your mother's saris and polishes his toenails pink, you tell yourself his transition is no longer a temporary one. He's still grieving, a relative says. Let him be.

One day, in the bedroom, you notice him blinking his kohl-lined eyes, the sparkle of your mother's Mangal sutra on his neck bobbing a flash on the walls.

What're you doing? you bawl.

He shrugs, applies a coral lipstick on his dark, thin lips and smacks them together. His hands look worn and you wonder if they can cook fluffy puris and bouncy Gulab jamuns, feel warm against your cheek, any time of the day.

Late that afternoon, he's changing into her silk blouse and you realize you've been wearing the same clothes every day. You look at his face—it's covered in foundation. The sari tied around his paunch and over his skinny legs has thin, pinned pleats. The little curly hairs on his arms and big toes are gone.

He asks you to watch your mother's favorite cooking show with him. Chickpea curry and bhaturas. He says he'll try the recipe. On the show, the fermented bread puffs in the fuming oil. A new old kind of transformation.

When do we distribute her ashes in the Ganges? you ask, your mind going straight to the urn.

He clears his throat. Her golden bangles on his arm jingle. We don't need to, he says, creating anxiety as you imagine your mother swimming in his veins, blooming, rising behind the whites of his eyes, wanting to come out, wanting to stay in.

from ATTICUS REVIEW

SNOWSTORM
TARA ISABEL ZAMBRANO

The snowstorm sends us home early from work, so we fuck and sleep. When we wake, the power is out and the room is a dark hole. We slip into sweatpants and over-sized shirts, pull up the shades to let in all that light reflected from white. The walls of the house seem thin, shivering. There are sounds we've seldom heard before—the wood cracking, as if giving up, a constant drip of water from the roof. We sit on the couch—tucked together under a blanket like children watching a scary movie. I say my mother lost me once on a crowded bus stop; you say you ran away from home, twice, and came back after a day. All along you'd been hiding in the attic. I say my parents stopped trimming my nails after my brother died. You say you were molested on a train, by a man your father's age. Then we go quiet; find our way through the dark to light the stove, make hot chocolate. I gulp the whole thing and want another immediately. Afterwards, I run my fingers over my crudely cut toenails. You reach an arm around my waist, suggest going back to bed. It feels like a good decision because there's nothing else to do except watch the snow that falls relentlessly, burying everything we've worked so hard for.

TARA ISABEL ZAMBRANO works as a semiconductor chip designer in a startup. Her work has been published in *Tin House* Online, *The Southampton Review*, *Slice*, *Bat City Review*, *Yemassee* and others. She is Assistant Flash Fiction Editor at Newfound.org. Tara moved from India to the United States two decades ago and holds an instrument rating for single engine aircraft. She lives in Texas. Website: taraisabelzambrano.wixsite.com/website

BRAINDRAIN
C PAM ZHANG

Because bodies couldn't cross the borders—bodies were unwanted. Bodies had disease and sweat and threatening biceps and strange-tongued languages, needed beds and jobs and maybe even women and lives, meant a future of preexisting bodies diluted by the sweat-flesh-stink-color of new bodies. No bodies. But what *was* okay, they said (they on the right side of the wall), was brains.

Tossed over, slipped through cracks too narrow for shoulders, bobbing across seas like coconuts, came the brains. At first border-residents complained of cerebral goo, which left a troubling smell of stale tears. A severe proclamation was issued. Thereafter, all brains were carefully wiped before being thrown, flown, slid, shipped, given.

Wondrous things arose from the brains. Congratulations and medals were handed around, one suited man on a podium to another. Because without bodies—their distracting skins, breasts, eyes, tongues—the ingenuity of brains could be fully harnessed for the first time. Within the walls, technology thrived. Money hummed.

Without, families sat around the bodies of loved ones. Hugged the slumped shoulders, bathed the hollow heads. Pressed the slack fingers to phones to authorize digital payments trickling in. No thanks exchanged. What was the point? The brains dwelled elsewhere.

C PAM ZHANG'S debut novel, *How Much Of These Hills Is Gold*, is forthcoming from Riverhead Books. She's been published in *American Short Fiction*, *Kenyon Review*, *McSweeney's Quarterly*, *Tin House*, and elsewhere. Born in Beijing and an artifact of many American cities, she now lives in San Francisco.

THE MICROVIEW
WITH ETGAR KERET

Because his influence on microfiction is unmistakable, the co-editors welcomed the opportunity to conduct a brief interview with Etgar Keret, the internationally-known Israeli author of such best-selling story collections as *Missing Kissinger*, *The Bus Driver Who Wanted to be God*, and most recently, *Cheap Moon* and *Suddenly a Knock on the Door*.

> **To begin, our readers would almost unanimously like to know how you "operate" when writing stories. Do you think about length when you begin?**

When I begin writing a story I usually know one thing: a certain thing that will happen in it, something about the character or the place in which it will take place. Writing a story is, for me, very much like following a thread. When you write, you don't execute, you discover.

> **Because many of the stories are so brief, how do you avoid anticipating the arc of the story too soon? Do you have specific revision strategies for your shortest pieces, sometimes even ways to make them shorter still?**

For me a short story is much harder to anticipate because you know very little about its universe when you begin writing it and by the time you understand it better the story is already finished.

> **You've said that storytelling has a feeling of intimacy, something that seems inherently true, but could you elaborate on that? If that feeling is absent as you write, do you set the story aside or even abandon it?**

When you write you are trying to say something. And if you have this special chance to share your thoughts and feeling with a reader then they might as well be genuine. What's the point in writing something that doesn't represent your emotions and thoughts in any way?

> **Another observation you have made is that your "enemy," when you write a story, is "the force of inertia." Could you speak to the ways in which you are attempting to push your audience to re-examine themselves or the world around them?**

In every story's plot there is always some default option. It is usually not the first idea to come to your head but the second one. The first idea is, many times, very authentic, sometimes totally enigmatic and we tend to discard it and then the second one, at least in my case, is something predictable and not necessarily authentic, the kind of thing that appears in our story not because it is true and unique but because it is semi-obvious.

This anthology will be published in English. What experiences have you had with translators of your work? Can you describe what it feels like to read your own work in translation?

A translator, in a sense, rewrites the story he translates because different languages work in different ways and you can't impose a story on a new language without recreating it a little. Even if it is mostly in an unconscious way.

It seems likely that your work would often produce some political conjecture. Has that occurred? If so, could you cite a story that has received such a response?

I think that my most controversial story was "shoes" which is a story about a child who receives a pair of Adidas sneakers from Germany and who, because of some misunderstanding, believes that those sneakers are made out of the skin of his grandfather who had died in the Holocaust. For me, it was a story about a child who tries to connect, through his new sneakers, with the memory of a grandfather he had never met. I've heard that when this story entered the high school curriculum in Israel there were some teachers who refused to teach it, thinking the story was disrespectful toward the memory of the Holocaust.

As a follow-up, is there a connection between fabulist content and the violence you might witness in Tel Aviv? Does Fabulism or Magic Realism allow you to express a certain state of being that Realism could not?

I don't necessarily see a connection between magic realism and violence but fantasy is always a way to transcend the reality you live in and, at times, to protest against it.

How did you come to discover your way of storytelling, especially often writing "short"? Were your influences Israeli or international?

The story that had influenced me the most and which had made me want to write was Kafka's Metamorphosis. When I read the story it had felt as if this story was about something I knew, almost as if it was written personally for me. It had made me want to write.

BETWEEN THE LINES

ROBERT SCOTELLARO

Co-Editor, "New Micro" (W.W. Norton & Co., 2018)

Having read thousands of micro-stories while co-editing an anthology of them with James Thomas for W. W. Norton, I was continually taken by the power in these small stories—the elegant, vigorous, nuanced, fresh language; the real/surreal, poetic or narrative prose—by the dynamism built into them lingering long after the last note was struck. It is an exciting time for the genre.

To better understand what something is, it is sometimes useful to establish what it is not. Microfiction is not fiction's equivalent of haiku (that singular microscopic focus on a fixed moment). Nor are these miniature stories fictive fragments, truncated versions of stories that would be magnificent if only they were longer.

Certainly, the literature has not been crafted for readers with short attention spans (whittled down by the rapidity of a technological age). And though it is true that with the proliferation of smart phones we've become accustomed to "quick fixes," this does not account for microfiction's expansive appeal, or explain why the form has flourished for millennia.

What makes these stories (400 words or less) so gripping, giving them an international popularity that is stunning?

I feel that a good deal of microfiction's power lies in that fertile territory between the lines, where that which is "unspoken" lives. Where a broader story is imparted via allusion and there is an implication that something deeper, more expansive is at stake.

This is akin to what author Grant Faulkner aptly posits: "What if instead of relying on the words of a story, I relied on the spectral spaces around those words?" What is implied, when finely crafted, can create a tacit partnering between writer and reader. It creates a world of what can be imagined.

Possibilities, drawn in very few words by skilled microfiction writers, can resonate exponentially. These pieces can be uniquely impactful, so much larger than their physical construct. Author Richard Bausch addresses this most eloquently: "When a story is compressed, the matter of it tends to require more size: that is, in order to make it work in so small a space its true subject must be proportionately larger."

Microfiction is multifaceted, fully realized, and satisfying. A form that is being published prolifically by quality magazines, anthologies, and presses today. It is being penned by a plethora of talented writers lending their skills to the form with a vast variety of approaches.

This is a fine book of microfiction: a compilation of the year's best. These are small, arresting stories that cut right to the heart of the matter, demonstrating that a story well told, no matter how small, expands beyond the space it inhabits. What lies beyond is very large indeed.

BEST MICROFICTION THANKS THE JOURNALS
WHERE THESE PIECES APPEARED IN 2018.
ALL MATERIAL USED BY PERMISSION.

"Even the Christmas Tree was Nicer That Year" by Valerie Fox from *Across the Margin*.

"A Brief History of Time in Our House" by Steven John from *Ad Hoc Fiction*.

"Lessons from my Mother" by Prosper Makara from *Afreada—Africa's Literary Magazine*.

"Boom" by Michael Martone from *Always Crashing*.

"Domestic" by Belinda Rimmer from *Anti-Heroin Chic*.

"A Roman Road" by Adam McOmber, "Half Tank" by Benjamin Woodard, and "Snowstorm" by Tara Isabel Zambrano from *Atticus Review*.

"Final Girl Slumber Party" by Meghan Phillips from *Barrelhouse*.

"The Delicate Art of Ikebana" by Cathy Ulrich from *Barren Magazine*.

"Northern Lights" by Tim Craig, "Things Left And Found By The Side Of The Road" by Jo Gatford, "Siren" by Fiona J. Mackintosh, "Satin Nightwear for Women Irregular" by Elisabeth Ingram Wallace, and "Mr Rochester and I" by Olga Dermott-Bond from *Things Left And Found At The Side Of The Road, Bath Flash Fiction Volume Three*, Ad Hoc Fiction.

"The Hair Child" by Kaj Tanaka from *Bending Genres*.

"Breathless" by Paul Luikart from *Brilliant Flash Fiction*.

"Niños de La Tierra" by José Enrique Medina from *Burnside Review*.

"The Seeds of Things" by Joe P. Squance from *Cease, Cows*.

"Sanctus Spiritus, 1512" by Sarah Arantza Amador, "Fragments of Evolution" by Cavin Gonzalez, "I Wanna Be Adored" by Melissa Goode, and "It's Shaped like a Grin, They Say" by KC Mead-Brewer from *Cheap Pop*.

"Any Body" by Sarah Freligh and "Not Sorry" by Sarah Salway from *Cincinnati Review*.

"This Weekend" by Tracy Lynne Oliver from *Fanzine*.

"The Laundry Room Comes First" by Charmaine Wilkerson from *Fiction Southeast*.

"The Chemistry of Living Things" by Fiona J. Mackintosh from *Fish Publishing*.

"He, She, It, They" by Anita Arlov, "An Inheritance" by Lutivini Majanja, and "What I Now Know" by Rachel Smith from *Flash Frontier*.

"Plum Jam" by Frances Gapper, "Frau Roentgen's Left Hand" by Anita Goveas, and "There Will Be No Lace" by TM Upchurch from *Flashback Fiction*.

"Self Portrait with Early December" by Page Leland from *Former Cactus*.

"Empire of Light" by Melissa Goode from *Gone Lawn*.

"Euthanasia" by Myfanwy Collins from *Jellyfish Review*.

"LifeColor Indoor Latex Paints® — Whites and Reds" by Kristen Ploetz from *JMWW*.

"You Can Find Joy in Doing Laundry" by Kathleen McGookey and "Swimming in Circles" by Roberta Beary from *KYSO Flash*.

"Reverse Field Trip" by Luke Wortley and "Bone Words" by Beth Gilstrap from *Longleaf Review*.

"Let's Sing All the Swear Words We Know" by Anita Goveas from *Lost Balloon*.

"Knock Knock" by Jessica Barksdale, "And Sometimes We Meet" by Dina Relles, "World's Finest" by Kim Samsin, and "My Father's Girlfriend" by Leonora Desar from *Matchbook Lit Mag*.

"A post-traumatic god" by Heather McQuillan and "Glossectomy" by Rachel Smith from *Meniscus*.

"Making an Illegal U Turn on 15th near Union" by Zach VandeZande from *Monkeybicycle*.

"Breathlessness" by Claire Polders from *Moonpark Review*.

"Candlelight and Flowers" by Tetman Callis from *NY Tyrant*.

"Feeding Time" by Tara Isabel Zambrano from *Okay Donkey*.

"Baby Dolls" by Becky Robison from *Pank*.

"Braindrain" by C Pam Zhang from *Paper Darts*.

"Training" by Michael Chin, "Missing" by Meghan Lamb, and "Abstinence Only" by Meghan Phillips from *Passages North*.

"You've Stopped" by Tommy Dean, "Becky" by Beth Gilstrap, and "Desert Motel" by Brad Rose from *Pithead Chapel*.

"Birdhouse" by Gregory Brown from *PRISM International*.

"The Monkey" by Leonora Desar, "Helping" by Clare Weze, and "My Father Comforts Me in the Form of Birds" by Sharon Telfer from *Reflex Fiction*.

"Health Care" by Dick Bentley from *Serving House Journal*.

"The Strip Club" by Will Finlayson and "Tsunami" by Elizabeth Stix from *Southampton Review*.

"The Central Line Has Severe Delays" by Jamie Thunder from *Spelk*.

"Kanekalon" by Raven Leilani from *Split Lip*.

"The End of the World" by Noa Sivan and "Princesses" by Xenia Taiga from *Synaesthesia Magazine*.

"11.37" by Peter Krumbach from *The Adroit Journal*.

"Crumbs" by Nicole Rivas from *The Cincinnati Review*.

"He Died We Left Him Til Morning" by Christopher Gaumer from *The Citron Review*.

"Klaus Weber, Curb House Numberer" by Michael Martone and "The Extinction Museum: Exhibit

#28 (incandescent bulb, unlit)" by Tina May Hall from *The Collagist*.

"New Old" by Tara Isabel Zambrano from *The Southampton Review*.

"Fire, Ocean" by Leonora Desar from *TSS*. "Masculinities" by Paul Strohm from *West Marin Review*.

"The Hungerer" by Matt Bell, "Tonight, We Are Awake" by Melissa Goode, "Not the Whole Story" by Toni Halleen, "A Warm Motherly Look" by Robert Lopez, "Loop-the-Loop" by Dan Malakoff, and "After the Flood Waters Came" by Dominica Phetteplace from *Wigleaf*.